A Blessing in Disguise

The Amish Lantern Mystery Series, Volume 5

Mary B. Barbee

Mystic Valley Press

This is a work of fiction. All of the characters, organizations, and events portrayed in this novel are either products of the author's imagination or are used fictitiously.

Editing Team: Molly Misko and Jenny Raith

Cover Design: Zahra Hassan

www.marybbarbee.com

To all the blessings in my life, especially to those that were in disguise.

Count it all joy, brothers, when you meet trials of various kinds, for you know that the testing of your faith produces steadfastness.

James 1:2

Chapter One

T he sun was setting in the Autumn sky and a brisk chill hung in the air. Four men gathered around the picnic table situated next to a simple white farmhouse, built with a wraparound porch. The men looked similar, wearing plain clothing and wide-brimmed hats, almost as if they were wearing uniforms. Three of the men were older gentlemen with long beards, and the other was clean-shaven and much younger than the rest.

Gabriel Lee pulled his coat closed and buttoned the top button near his neck. He was ready for this meeting to adjourn, but he sat patiently next to his father without complaint, listening closely to the conversation among the men. Growing up the son of the community's deacon, he was no stranger to the Amish proverb: *Remember, when you talk, you only repeat what you already know; if you listen, you might learn something.*

"There's one more thing I wanted to discuss tonight, Bishop," Deacon Lee cleared his throat before continuing. "I want to talk about Matthew Beiler and his relationship with the *Englischer* woman who owns the diner."

Bishop Packer exhaled a long slow breath as the other men sat in silence, waiting for his response. "*Jah*, it's no surprise that you want to discuss that, Deacon. You've kept no secret about where you stand with Matthew dating Ms. McLean, but it's getting late." He gestured toward the orange sherbet colored sky.

Minister Brandenburger quickly interjected, "I agree with the bishop. Dinner will be *gut* and cold by the time I get home."

Gabriel could feel his father's discontent without so much as a glance his way.

"Well, when do you expect to stop this nonsense?" Deacon Lee demanded an answer as he pushed the palms of his hands down on the table and leaned forward toward the bishop and the minister. "I mean, besides the fact that she is an *Englischer*, the woman has been married before! It's preposterous that you are even considering letting this go on, Bishop. I am the deacon of this community, and I'll remind you that I am to be the one to announce the marriages." The deacon continued ranting, "And I don't agree with it. I think it's too liberal, and I don't want to support it." The words rushed out of his mouth as if he had been holding them inside for too long.

Bishop Packer stood and arched his back, stretching before he responded. He spoke his words slowly and deliberately. "I have heard what you have to say, Deacon, but I have spoken with Matthew at great length about this already."

Minister Brandenburger picked up where Deacon Lee left off. "Bishop, I have to say that I haven't got Matthew's baptism on the calendar yet, either. How can we be sure that he is following the *Ordnung* and living a life of obedience to *Gotte*?" He lifted one eyebrow as he presented his own suspicions. He had clearly pushed his soon-to-be cold dinner out of his mind.

"We can't be sure," Deacon Lee insisted. "That is exactly what I am saying. You must meet with Matthew again, Bishop, and put an end to this. The entire community could be in danger."

Bishop Packer scoffed. "How do you think Matthew and Jessica's relationship could put the rest of us in danger, exactly, Deacon? You're overreacting."

"We can't trust them, Bishop."

"Who can't we trust, Deacon?" Bishop Packer implored. "How easily you forget. The *Englischers* have helped us in times of need in the recent past. When my own young daughter was taken, the sheriff showed great kindness through that horrible experience."

Deacon Lee nodded and cast his eyes down at the tabletop.

"And the townsfolk also diligently purchase our goods at the market and in our stores," the bishop continued.

Gabriel sat and listened, but he yearned to make his father proud of him, and he wanted to help solidify his father's stance. He politely interjected, "With all due respect, Bishop Packer, I think my *dat* is remembering the fires that were started by the *Englischers* not long after the horrible event with your daughter. Not to mention how every time there is a crime, it seems that it is our men that are first to be accused."

Deacon Lee rested his hand on his son's shoulder and nodded his agreement and approval.

"I am afraid that you are not joined by many of us, Bishop, in your opinion that what is happening right under our noses is ok," the deacon said in a calm voice.

The bishop nodded. "I am aware," he said matter-of-factly, "but I don't believe we are going to come to any conclusion tonight, nor do we need to. The sky is dark, and we all need to go home to be with our families."

Minister Brandenburger stood and said, "Let us bow our heads in a final prayer, then, shall we?"

The bishop and the deacon nodded in agreement, and all bowed their heads as the minister began reciting his quiet prayer.

"Dear *Gotte*, we trust in you to keep us from harm and illuminate the path which we should take. We put our confidence in you, Dear Lord, to provide for our wonderful community and to keep us safe." He paused.

"Amen," the men said quietly in unison.

"Now let us head home to where it is warm and get some rest for our busy days tomorrow," the bishop said, tipping his hat and nodding his head to each of the men.

"*Jah, gut* night to you, Bishop" Deacon Lee said, mimicking his motions. "We shall continue this discussion another time."

"That we will," Bishop Packer said as he turned to head inside his house.

Minister Brandenburger, Deacon Lee and Gabriel walked away together towards their neighboring homes.

"I worry that we won't be able to get through to him," Deacon Lee said, shaking his head.

Minister Brandenburger was quiet and pushed his hands into his pocket, shrugging his shoulders as if to protect his neck from the cold.

"It's clearly not resolved," Gabriel said, walking beside his father, matching his stride. "I am not sure the bishop is going to do anything different, *Dat*. We might have to take matters into our own hands."

Minister Brandenburger stopped abruptly. Deacon Lee and Gabriel stopped as well, and the three men formed a small circle in the middle of the dirt road.

"What are you saying, Gabriel? Bishop Packer confirmed that we will discuss it further another time." The only light was from the bright moon, and it cast enough of a glow across the minister's face that Gabriel could see the look of concern directed toward him.

Gabriel opened his mouth to respond, but his father squeezed his arm and interrupted. "I think my son meant exactly what he said. We might have to take matters into our own hands," he paused. "And that could begin with a tough conversation with Matthew, of course. I don't see anything wrong with just talking to him, do you, Minister?"

Minister Brandenburger shook his head and uttered, "No, I suppose you're right. Gabriel's words just sounded a bit harsh, and I just want to make sure we do not stray from the principles on which our faith is founded."

Gabriel stepped forward out of his father's shadow and spoke directly to the minister, his voice calm and steady. "For sure and certain, Minister Brandenburger. I would hope you know that I wouldn't do anything to bring shame to the community. I have never done anything in the past to cause any trouble, have I?"

The minister took a half step back but maintained eye contact with Gabriel in the moonlight. "*Vell*, no, of course not," he said. He adjusted his hat on his head and took a breath. After an uncomfortable moment of silence, he said, "It's late now, *bruders*, and this conversation is starting to feel overdone. Let's just make our way home and enjoy the rest of the evening." He gestured for the deacon and his son to follow him as he began to pick up the pace down the road.

"*Jah*, it is a beautiful night, isn't it, *sohn*?" Deacon Lee asked Gabriel as he guided him by the arm to fall back in line with the minister on the walk home.

"Mmhmm," Gabriel muttered in agreement. He was distracted. He worked tirelessly to earn his father's respect, and he wondered if he had accomplished that this evening. He planned to let his father know that he wasn't just talking. He would help his father put an end to Matthew Beiler's relationship if it came to that, and he looked forward to the opportunity to prove his worth. He shook his head as if to clear his thoughts and focused again on matching his father's stride as the three men turned off the road and proceeded down a walking path into the night.

Chapter Two

The smell of bacon and eggs drifted through the kitchen and Anna Miller's stomach growled. "I don't know why I'm so hungry this morning," Anna said to Eli as she set a breakfast casserole in the middle of the table.

"We both slept later than usual," Eli said, reaching for the small plate of butter. "I think the changing season sends us into some strange sort of hibernation as we get older."

"*Jah*, that may be true," Anna said. "I guess we are just turning into two old bears," she chuckled.

There was a soft knock at the back door as it pushed open slowly. Anna's sister, Beth, entered, carrying a tray piled high with cinnamon rolls. "*Gut mariye!*" she sang out as she wrapped one arm around her sister's shoulders for a gentle squeeze.

"*Gut mariye, Schwester,*" Anna grinned, leaning into Beth's quick hug. She recognized the *kapp* her sister was wearing as one that Beth had borrowed a few weeks ago but had not yet returned. Anna's oldest daughter Sarah had crafted and gifted it to her for Christmas the year before, but even though it was one of her favorites, she didn't mind that her sister was wearing it. Beth and Anna were identical twins and shared almost everything. They were sisters and best friends. Some might say the two women were practically the same person, but those closest to them could easily tell them apart.

Anna was born just a few minutes before Beth, and she naturally stepped into the older sister role whenever life called for it. Beth struggled with high-functioning autism, and although her diagnosis wasn't public knowledge, she struggled with little things in life that are often taken for granted. In Beth's world, everything needed to be in order and things were most often seen as black or white. Anna had become accustomed to Beth's "quirks," as they referred to them, remaining patient and taking no offense when Beth would rearrange her settings on the dinner table or adjust the curtains so they sat the same distance on each side of the window. She also fell into a caretaker role whenever Beth would become overwhelmed with anxiety or when Beth's stress levels would sink into what could seem like unending spirals of thought. She loved her sister dearly, and the feelings were mutual.

"Is Noah joining us this morning?" Anna asked.

Beth nodded. "*Jah*, he is right behind me. How are you two doing this morning? It is going to be such a beautiful day today!" Beth set the tray of cinnamon rolls next to the breakfast casserole and took a seat on Eli's left, after greeting him with a quick pat on the shoulder. Eli welcomed Beth with a warm smile.

"*Gut, gut,*" Eli said. "Anna and I were just talking about..." Eli's sentence was interrupted as Noah walked in the door.

"*Gut mariye*, Anna and Eli," Noah said cheerfully. "It's a beautiful day outside!"

Eli and Anna chuckled. "That's what your *fraa* was just saying, Noah. *Wilkumme!* Come have a seat. We slept a little bit later this morning, and I just heard Anna's stomach growling." He grinned at his wife as she took the seat to his right, across from Beth.

Beth agreed. "I slept later than normal as well, although Noah was up at his usual early time. I was saying that it must be the cooler Autumn mornings that are causing me to sleep so much harder than usual." Noah settled next to Beth. Anna began serving a large spoonful of casserole onto each plate. Beth's similar thoughts were not lost on Eli and Anna as they exchanged a quick knowing smile between them.

Noah thanked Anna for the casserole before saying, "The two of you are usually up before the sun, baking away. I think it's ok to treat yourself to a lazy morning every once in a while. Your health is important, and if your body needs the extra hour of sleep, then you should have it."

Eli grinned, "*Jah*, I agree with Noah. An occasional sleep-in is to be expected after everything the two of you do for us and for the family."

"And for the community," Noah added.

"You're both very kind," Beth said, winking at Anna. "Speaking of the community, Anna, you and I should start planning the Thanksgiving dinner party. People are starting to ask if we had any ideas of the time and place, or who is to bring what."

Anna had expected Beth to mention the upcoming holiday dinner event today. If there was one thing that Beth loved to do more than anything, it was party planning. "*Jah*, I saw Rebecca the other day, and she mentioned how excited she was to have a community-wide celebration this year. She was wanting to sign up to bring her wonderful sweet potato pie." Anna set the serving spoon down into the half-empty casserole dish.

Eli interjected. "Let's thank *Gotte* for our food," he said, as he bowed his head and folded his hands in front of him. Noah and the sisters did the same.

"Father, thank you for the gifts of nourishment on our table in front of us this morning. May it bring us good health and the energy to do your work on this beautiful day. Amen." Eli spoke quietly.

"Amen," Anna, Beth and Noah said in agreement before diving into their meals.

"So, Thanksgiving dinner will be a bit different from last year, eh?" Noah said. "I enjoy our intimate time with all the children and grandchildren, and nieces and nephews, but of course, I always look forward to community-wide celebrations, too. It seems as if life gets so busy around here that we don't gather as a community as often as we used to anymore."

"*Jah*, and we need that," Eli said. "The community does not seem as close as we once were."

"Really? I wonder why you think that, Eli? We have so much to be thankful for this year," Anna was genuinely surprised at Eli's comment.

"Oh, yes, that is so true. So many reasons for gratitude, especially this year. Is that what you meant, Eli?" Beth asked between bites.

"*Vell*, I have noticed a slight tension among the men. There seems to be some underlying disagreement about some things," Eli said. Anna knew her husband was hesitant to discuss this sort of thing. He made a strong effort to show respect and to avoid gossip.

"I think I know what you mean, Eli," Noah chimed in. "I picked up on a little bit of that after Sunday's service even."

"*Ach du lieva*, if there were arguments just after service, we have bigger problems than you're letting on," Beth said. With one look, Anna could sense that Beth was beginning to panic and may be jumping to conclusions, assuming that the community was doomed to fall apart. Anna was concerned by the comments, too, but she really didn't want Beth to be upset.

"Hold on now before you get all excited, *Schwester*," Anna said with a soft comforting voice. "Eli and Noah only said there was some slight tension. That is to be expected as a bit of blowback after everything the community has been through this year. It's no surprise there is still some healing needed, and that is exactly why we need this upcoming celebration. There is nothing more healing than gathering for the purpose of gratitude, wouldn't you say?"

Beth exhaled the breath she had been holding and nodded her head. Anna watched as Beth's face relaxed, and a warmth returned to her eyes. "You're right, *Schwester*.

There is a lot riding on this gathering. We will make sure it is perfect," Beth said with a small smile.

"Now, nothing has to be perfect, *lieb*," Noah said, "but I'm sure it will be as wonderful as every other party the two of you have planned and hosted." He took a bite of his casserole. "I'm looking forward to it already."

Eli nodded, "Oh, me too. I'm also really looking forward to it." He changed the subject. "This breakfast casserole is as good as ever, Anna. I could eat way more than I should," he said, setting his fork down on his empty plate.

"Well, I hope you saved some room for Beth's cinnamon rolls. She is trying out a new recipe, right, Beth?" Anna asked. Her voice was nonchalant, but she was hiding the worry in her mind. She knew that Beth was still caught up in her thoughts and wrought with worry over the suggestion that people in the community were sitting in contempt with each other. And she could admit that she wasn't alone. She wondered what Eli was referring to and was anxious to get him alone to question him further about his off-the-cuff comment. She would assess if it was serious and fill Beth in appropriately.

Beth nodded, "*Jah*, that's right. They are ginger carrot cake cinnamon rolls. I baked them last night and frosted them with cream cheese frosting this morning before heading over here. I will be interested to see what you all think." She grabbed the plate and held it steady for Eli, "Are you up for trying something new this morning, *bruder*?"

Eli selected a roll from the top of the pile. "Of course I am. When have I ever turned down a goodie?" He grinned.

"I'd say that you and I could be the luckiest men around, Eli, to have these two smart and talented women in our lives," Noah said between bites.

Eli nodded in agreement and closed his eyes, humming as he tasted the first bite of the scrumptious pastry.

Anna laughed, "Well, I guess that's the best compliment you could get, *Schwester*."

Beth's smile spread across her face, and Anna could tell all was right again. "I'll try one!" Anna announced as she reached for a smaller roll on the side of the tray.

"Me too," said Noah, and Beth placed rolls on her and Noah's plates, as well.

Everyone proceeded to enjoy their dessert and compliment the chef before Beth and Anna rose to clear the table and clean the dishes. Eli and Noah remained seated at the table discussing the weather, Eli's farming chores ahead of him, preparing for winter, and Noah's busy day at the shop.

"So, after you get Noah out the door, do you want to come back over and we can start planning the party?"

Anna asked Beth, wiping a freshly washed plate dry with a dishcloth.

"Absolutely," Beth said, running a soapy plate under the water to rinse it. "I have to go to the grocery store later, as well, if you want to come with me," she said.

Anna smiled at her sister. "I would like nothing better than to spend the day with my sister, you know that," she said, handing Beth the towel to dry her hands.

"What would we do, Anna, if we didn't build our houses right next to each other?" Beth asked, jokingly.

"Well, I guess I would have to learn how to drive a buggy," Anna responded with a wink.

"Oh, thank goodness you don't have to do that!" Beth said, teasing her sister. Laughter filled the room.

Chapter Three

Jessica McLean slid the door of the pastry case open and turned to grab a small porcelain dessert plate from the shelf behind her. She did a quick inventory of the goodies that were left after the lunch rush and used a set of tongs to grab the last piece of pumpkin pie cake, placing it gingerly on the plate.

"Nice place you got here," a man's voice seemed to come out of nowhere.

The voice startled her, and the metal tongs clanged loudly as they hit the floor. James McLean, Jessica's ex-husband, stood on the other side of the counter dressed in a stylish navy-blue suit and crisp white shirt. His blonde hair was cut short on the sides with tamed waves on the top that added at least an inch or two to his height.

Jessica was speechless. She had not laid eyes on James in over five years and was shocked to see him standing on the other side of the front counter in her diner.

"Oh, my gosh, James," she said after recovering. "What are you doing here?"

"Well, hello to you, too," James said with a broad smile.

Jessica felt her face grow warm. She was immediately uncomfortable. She found herself searching for something to say next, but nothing came to mind.

James continued to stand there with a grin. "Well, it's good to see you, Jess. You don't look a day older," he said, taking a seat on a stool at the bar.

Jessica composed herself as she set the plate down and bent over to pick up the tongs. "Seriously, James, why are you here?" She asked again, washing the tongs in the sink.

James's eyes were the color of the ocean and they twinkled as he sat quietly, watching Jessica wash and then dry the metal tongs. He finally answered the question. "Well, I came to see you, of course. I mean, I can't think of another good reason why I'd drive all the way out to Little Valley, can you?"

Jessica's jaw set, and her eyes grew cold. "I have to serve this to my customers," Jessica managed to utter. She grabbed the cake, two forks and the fresh pot of coffee from behind the counter and made a beeline for the table by the window.

"Totally fine. I'll wait right here for ya," James said as she walked away.

Jessica's heart was racing as she delivered the dessert and refilled her customers' coffee cups. "Can I get you anything else?" She asked. *Please, please need something else,* she thought. The couple were the only customers in the diner, and the last thing she wanted was to be alone with her ex-husband.

James and Jessica had fallen madly in love and married too quickly when they were both young, just out of high school. But, a few years into the marriage, they realized their physical attraction to each other had been the only real thing they shared. It turned out that they were very different people, with different dreams and aspirations, and simply couldn't see eye to eye on so many lifestyle choices. They had managed to stay together for a total of ten very long years, much longer than they probably should have. Their divorce was drawn out and dramatic, and Jessica had hoped they had parted ways for good. She would have been perfectly fine never seeing James's pretty face again.

"No, thank you. This looks wonderful," the woman at the table said before continuing her conversation with the man across from her. The couple appeared to be in their mid to late twenties, and Jessica recognized the excitement and anticipation on the young woman's face. She fought the urge to interrupt, grab her by the shoulders and firmly say to her, "snap out of it!"

Instead, she responded, "Ok, great. Well, enjoy your cake and just holler if you need me then."

Returning to the counter, Jessica hoped that her face hid the worry that she felt. She set the coffee pot back on the element before turning to face him.

She stood there silent and pushed her hands into the pockets of her apron, but she pushed her shoulders back and stood tall. She recently read in a book on personal development how if you stand like a superwoman, you'll feel more confident and stronger. This was the perfect time to give that a try.

"Well, aren't you going to offer me a coffee or some of that cake?" James said. Jessica knew he was enjoying this. She knew James like the back of her hand, and it wasn't unlike him to play the friendly card while holding onto an ulterior motive.

Jessica took a slow deep breath. "I don't wanna offer you coffee, James. I'm not gonna pretend I'm happy to see you, if that's what you're hoping," she said, her voice low so as not to make a scene.

James pretended to grab his heart in pain and squeezed his eyes shut, wrinkling his smooth ageless forehead.

"Aah," he moaned dramatically, "I'm hurt, Jessica." He laughed and after his quick attempt at acting, he dropped his hand on the counter and continued, "I thought you *might* be as glad to see me as I am to see you."

"Why would I be glad to see you, James?" Jessica said, wringing out a cloth and wiping the counter in front of him. "I said my final goodbye years ago, and I've moved on." She stopped and held his gaze, feeling her confidence resurfacing. "I'm happy now," she said, "and I can't imagine the real reason you're here. So just get to it so I can get on with my day."

"I told you," James said, "I've come to see you. And maybe to have a cup of Heaven's Diner's famous coffee." He gestured toward the coffee pot.

Jessica stood with her hand on her hip. She knew better than to trust James, and she suspected he was playing games. She took another deep breath and tried to summon the strength that she was going to need as his opponent.

"Fine," she said, as she turned her back to James and grabbed a clean coffee cup off the shelf. Setting it in front of him, she poured the dark steaming liquid. Knowing full well that he takes his coffee black, she placed a small set of creamer and sugar packs next to his cup.

James watched attentively as Jessica moved through the motions. "Thank you, Jess," he said. Maintaining eye contact, he raised the cup to his lips and took a sip. "So, how have you been?" He asked politely.

Jessica didn't answer. She began filling condiment bottles.

"My parents send their love," James continued. Jessica rolled her eyes. James was raised in the city in an affluent family, and although they were always cordial, it was no secret that Jessica was not their pick for their son.

Screwing the cap on the last bottle of ketchup, Jessica looked up and met James's eyes again. "James," she said, pausing briefly, "I don't want to do this. I'm not going to stand here and pretend like we're old friends."

"Aren't we, though?" James asked, "Old friends, I mean? We were in each other's lives for over ten years, Jess."

"Yeah, and it was terrible."

"Ah, it wasn't all terrible, was it, Jess?" James winked at Jessica, and she felt a cold chill run down her spine.

"Look, if you want to know the truth, Jess, here it is," James paused and set down his coffee cup. His smile disappeared and his eyes softened. "I miss you," he said, "and I've been thinking about you a lot."

Jessica wasn't moved by his words. "This must be a joke," she said, shaking her head. "Look, James, I don't know what kind of game you're playing here, but I don't have time for it. I've got a business to run." She glanced over at the customers who were still chatting with each other and still working on their shared piece of cake. She looked past them, out the large windows at the front of the diner, hoping that someone would walk in the door and save her from this conversation. She could see Matthew across the street setting up a new display of beautiful flowers on the front porch of his flower shop, The Secret Garden. She would give anything to be over there with him right now instead of standing here, face to face with her past.

James followed Jessica's line of sight. "Is that your new boyfriend out there?" He asked, his voice light and aloof.

Jessica whipped her head back to James, her eyes cold and narrowed. "I think you should go, James. You're wasting your time here," she said.

"But we haven't really had a chance to get caught up," James said, taking another slow sip of his coffee.

"We're not friends, James," Jessica repeated, hating the frustration in her tone.

James stared at Jessica for a long moment without moving, his face blank of expression. Jessica maintained the same, looking right back into his eyes. James finally shifted his eyes toward his coffee, lifted the cup to his lips and swallowed the last bit.

"That will be two dollars," Jessica said in an unfriendly voice.

Without a word, James pulled his wallet out of his pocket and dropped a twenty-dollar bill on the counter. "Keep the change," he said with another wink.

"Mind if I use your restroom before I go, or is it just reserved for friends?" James asked sarcastically, wiggling his fingers in the air to mimic quotations around the word friends.

Jessica sighed and pointed to the hallway. "It's in the hallway on your left," she said before picking up the twenty-dollar bill and slipping it in her apron pocket.

James nodded and headed toward the back as Jessica cleaned his cup and returned to the guests at the table. "How was the cake?" she asked the young couple.

"Oh, it was absolutely delicious!" the woman exclaimed. "Are you able to share the recipe? I've never had a pumpkin pie cake before, and I would love to make it for Thanksgiving."

Jessica smiled, "I'm afraid I'm not the baker. My dear friends, Anna Miller and Beth Troyer are the ones who supply the diner with baked goods," she said. "And I agree, it is really quite good. I can order a full cake for you to have for Thanksgiving, though, if you'd like," she offered.

"Yes, please! That would be wonderful," the young woman said, clasping her hands together in excitement.

As Jessica began taking down her information, they were interrupted by James calling out, one hand on the open door, "Thanks, again, for the hospitality, Ms. McLean! I'll see you next time!" he called out in a cheery voice before finally exiting.

Jessica, aware of the couple's eyes on her, lifted her hand to wave but did not respond. She watched out of the corner of her eye through the front window as James approached a cherry red Chevrolet Corvette, parked right on Main Street in front of Heaven's Diner.

She gasped as she saw James call out and raise his hand to wave to Matthew, still standing in front of his shop. Matthew smiled and tipped his hat to return his greeting.

"Is everything ok, Ms. McLean?" the customer asked, concerned.

Jessica quickly composed herself and waved her left hand in the air before shifting her eyes back down to her notepad, "Oh, yes, I'm fine. I'm so sorry about that. Let's see... what's your phone number again?"

Chapter Four

Jessica parked her car in the same parking spot on Main Street that she used every day, just to the left of Heaven's Diner. The sun was still rising in the sky, and the air was cool with an occasional sharp gust of wind. Stepping out of her car, Jessica pulled her cross-body purse strap over her head and tugged on her beanie until it fully covered her cold earlobes. She walked the familiar short path on the sidewalk to the front door of her diner. She was so proud of how much she had accomplished since moving to Little Valley and opening her restaurant. She had decided to turn the visit from James into a positive and welcome reminder of just how happy she had become over the past few years.

She wiggled the diner's keys out of the front pocket of her dark blue jeans and unlocked the door. Pushing the door open, she entered, reaching for the light switch on her right. Before her fingers could find the switch, she was propelled forward from a force behind her. Catching her balance, she turned and gasped. She tried to scream, but she felt as if she had suddenly lost her voice.

"Don't make a noise," the man standing face to face with Jessica said quietly with a stern voice.

Seconds later, Jessica found she was able to speak, but her voice shook as she asked, "What's happening?"

The man shut the door behind him and turned the lock. From the sunlight that slid between the slats of the window blinds, Jessica could see the man was wearing a light grey ski mask and dark clothing. He looked just an inch taller than her, but he sported a muscular intimidating build. Most importantly, she could see the streams of sunlight shimmer on the gun that was pointed directly at her chest. She froze in place. Every second felt like an eternity as she waited for an answer to her question.

The man gestured with the gun towards the cash register. "Go on," he said. His voice was rough and deep. "The back. I know you have a safe back there. I want what's in it."

Jessica nodded. *Did he really know that she had a safe in the back or was he bluffing,* she wondered, but she was not interested in arguing with him at all. Her legs felt like jello as she walked towards the storage room. She could hear his footsteps close behind her and could hear him breathing through the mask. Her mind began to race. *What if he intends to take what's in the safe and then kill me?* The thought crossed her mind, but she shooed it away quickly. The one lesson she had learned to put into practice daily since her marriage was to stop using the phrase *what if* in a sentence and to focus on the positive and on the present.

She reached the storage room and flipped on the lights. She headed toward the closed door of the small office tucked away at the back of the storage room, just past the shelves of canned goods. She stopped and turned to the man with the gun. "It's locked," she said. "I lock it every night. But I think I dropped my keys when you came in the door." She was fearful of how the masked man would react to this, but he lifted his free hand and dangled the keys just inches away from her face.

"Oh. Well, I guess you picked them up," Jessica said awkwardly. She was torn; on the one hand it would have been nice to be able to stall opening the safe, but on the other hand...her thoughts turned to Matthew. He would be setting up shop soon. She thought it was possible that he might notice that her car was parked out front, but the lights in the diner were still off and the blinds still drawn.

The last thing she wanted was for Matthew to come check on her and end up getting hurt. *No, it's best to give this guy what he wants and get him out of here*, she thought.

She gingerly reached out to take the keys and turned to unlock the office door. The old door creaked when she pushed it open. The office was a very small space, with only room for a desk pushed against the opposite wall from the doorway, a small chair with wheels, and a file cabinet turned sideways against the left wall. She reached over to turn on the desk lamp that sat on her neatly organized desk.

On the wall to her right was a large canvas painting of a vase of yellow roses that she had created when she was much younger and still in school. She hated that painting for many years. It reminded her of the painful years when her father left the family behind for a new life with his mistress. Jessica remembered how her mother had reacted to the painting when she brought it home. She cried when she saw it, exclaiming how talented Jessica was and how she would treasure it forever. She hung it over the mantle in the living room and showed it off to everyone who visited. It was after her mother had passed away that Jessica found the painting in her possession again, but this time, the strokes of paint resembled her mother's strength and love. She, too, considered it a treasure now, so it was an easy choice when it came time to select a canvas to help create a hiding place for her diner's wall safe.

Jessica stopped and looked back at the man. He was standing in the doorway of the office and waved his gun toward the painting. "Go on then," he said. "Hurry up," he snapped, cupping his free hand under the butt of the gun, arms stretched long so that the gun was now only inches away from Jessica's head.

Jessica's brows furrowed as she recognized that the man somehow knew the safe was behind the painting, but she didn't have time to analyze that further. She reached up and carefully removed the painting, revealing the wall safe.

"I don't honestly know how much cash I have in here," she said, as she turned the combination lock slowly to the right until it reached the number 3.

"I mean, I didn't go to the bank last night, so I know there's at least a thousand dollars or so in here from the past couple days." She turned the lock all the way to the left, passing the number and stopping on the number 2.

The man remained silent.

Making the final turn of the lock to the right and stopping on the number 8, Jessica could feel and hear the safe's lock unlatch. She opened the door to the safe and began to reach in. She would give the man the cash that she had stored away in the envelope, but she wouldn't reveal that her mother's precious diamond ring was tucked away

33

in the very back, wrapped in a small piece of velvet that she had cut from the seam of the gown her mother wore when she was laid to rest.

As she pulled out the envelope of cash, the man pushed her chest and face down onto the top of the desk. Her hands instinctively dropped the envelope and moved to her sides to cushion herself, her palms pressed against the desk. Her small frame was no contest to the man's strength. He leaned over her, his hand on her head and his elbow bearing into her upper back between her shoulder blades. Her head pounded. Her left cheek was pressed against the wood as she watched him slip his gun into the waistband of his pants and reach his free hand into the safe.

Jessica watched the small piece of emerald green velvet fall out of his hand carelessly as he examined the special ring.

"No, please," Jessica whimpered quietly. "You don't understand. That was my mother's ring."

"That's enough," he snapped at Jessica, gritting his teeth. He pushed the ring into his front pocket. "Where's the money?" She felt the cold barrel of the gun touch her cheek.

A tear escaped Jessica's right eye, crossed the bridge of her nose, and joined forces with a tear from her left eye before landing on the desk. In a defeated voice, she said quietly, "I don't know. I was handing it to you when you..." Her voice trailed off.

The man looked around and saw the envelope of cash lying on the floor. He released Jessica and grabbed the back of her shirt, pulling her into a standing position. "Pick up the envelope," he ordered.

Jessica nodded and bent down to collect the envelope, her hands visibly shaking. She stood and he promptly snatched it out of her hand, stuffing it into his pockets, as well.

"Show me the back door to this joint," he grumbled.

Jessica nodded. She was relieved to be leaving the small office space, but she was terrified of what was going to happen next. *Would he just let her go, or was the plan to kill her and then take off?*

She only used the back door whenever she was receiving larger deliveries of supplies which happened once or twice a month. Ironically, she never felt safe entering and exiting through the back door, so it remained locked most of the time. She had been organizing her storage room the past few days and had moved three twenty-pound bags of rice in front of the door. She apologized meekly as she began sliding the heavy bags out of the way so she could gain access for the armed man. He was breathing heavily, sighing as if he were frustrated it was taking her so long, but otherwise, he stood silent as he held the gun steady with Jessica as his target.

Jessica unlocked the deadbolt and the lock on the door handle and pushed the door open. She was greeted by the sun and fresh air, but she held her breath for what might happen next.

The man pushed past her and fled on foot, running towards the woods at the far right of the lot.

Jessica released a long breath as she leaned against the open door, slid to the ground and cried. Her head rested on her knees, and her shoulders shook as she sobbed loudly.

Chapter Five

After a few moments, Jessica pulled herself together and stood to her feet. She pulled the door shut, feeling weak behind the weight of the heavy door. With her hands trembling, she turned the lock on the door and wiped her face with her sleeve. She smoothed her hair and straightened her purse. *It's odd that he didn't take my purse*, she thought to herself.

Before heading to the phone to call the police, she turned on the overhead lights in the dining room and opened the blinds. She needed to let some more sunlight in to feel safe.

A knock at the front door almost made her squeal out loud. She jumped out of her skin, but she let out a sigh of relief when she saw Matthew's kind face through the glass door.

"Good morning, Jessica!" Matthew called out from the other side of the door in a cheery voice as she approached. As soon as she was close enough for Matthew to see her face clearly, his expression changed to one of worry.

"Jessica, are you okay?" He asked as she unlocked the door and pulled the door open. "What happened?"

"It was horrible, Matthew," she said, as her hand instinctively covered her mouth, and she lowered her eyes. Tears started to flow down her cheeks again.

Matthew entered the diner and closed the door behind him. "Oh, my goodness, is everything okay?" he asked as he touched her shoulder assuredly. He waited for her to continue.

She threw herself into his arms and wept on his shoulder. For a long few minutes, she couldn't speak through the tears. Then, she stood upright and after wiping her face with the back of her hands, she dropped her arms by her side.

"Matthew, I was robbed," she said quietly, her sad eyes gazing into his.

Matthew gasped. "What?!" He stammered, "But who? W-w-when?" He jumped into action and gently escorted her to a chair near the front door. "Shall I lock the front door for now?" he asked.

Jessica nodded. She watched as Matthew leapt to quickly lock the door and return to her side, pulling a chair over next to her and sitting just inches away. She slumped forward and he slowly rubbed her back, patiently waiting for her to explain what happened.

Jessica immediately felt safe again with Matthew there. She proceeded to tell Matthew how the masked man pushed open the door and took her money. Tears welled up in her eyes again as she remembered the ring, but she wasn't sure if she could handle telling that part of the story. She felt as if she would just fall to pieces.

"We have to call the police," Matthew said, rising to his feet.

"Yes, I was just about to do that when you arrived," she said. She stood slowly, her muscles still tense from the manhandling. Once behind the front counter, she reached down and grabbed the phone's receiver. She called the sheriff's office, and Deputy Christopher Jones answered the phone.

"Sheriff's office," Deputy Jones' husky morning voice greeted her.

"Hi, this is Jessica McLean from Heaven's Diner."

"Oh, good morning, Ms. McLean! This is Deputy Jones. How are you today?"

"Um, hi, Deputy," Jessica swallowed back tears. "I'm actually calling to report a robbery that just happened here at my diner."

The deputy's tone of voice immediately became concerned, "Oh, no! I'm so sorry that happened, Jessica. Are you okay? Are you safe now?"

Jessica stuttered. "I'm... I'm fine. I mean, I'm not hurt. He ran out the back door," she said. "But he had a gun," she paused, "and he stole what I had in my safe." She felt a tear fall down her face. Matthew, standing next to her, put his arm around her shoulders.

"The sheriff and I will head that way right now, Ms. McLean," the deputy responded. "Please try not to touch or move anything. We'll want to investigate everything."

Jessica nodded and then quietly said, "Okay, thank you," before hanging up the phone.

She looked at Matthew. "They're on their way," she said. Matthew nodded and slowly dropped his arm.

Jessica grabbed a tissue from a box of Kleenex on the shelf just below the counter and blew her nose. "I understand if you need to go open your shop," she said, realizing how much time had passed since she first slipped her keys in the lock outside the front of her diner.

Matthew shook his head, "No, ma'am. I'm not worried about that. Let me help you. What can I do?"

Jessica pulled the stool over and leaned against it. She felt defeated. She had no idea how she would open the diner and serve customers without breaking down, but the robber had just taken all her money and she knew it could put her in a financial bind to close the diner for the day. Her brow wrinkled and she looked up at Matthew, who stood, leaning against the counter, silently giving Jessica the space she needed to think.

"I honestly don't know what to do right now, Matthew," she said. She could feel the tears forming again, and it was making her frustrated. She wasn't one to cry all the time, but she felt the furthest from strong at that moment.

"Well, let's just wait for the sheriff to get here, and we'll go from there," Matthew suggested. "It's only just after eight o'clock right now. There's still an hour until you normally open for the day."

Jessica buried her face in her hands for a moment, then raising her face again, she blinked back more tears.

"I don't know if I am going to be able to open the diner today." Her voice cracked with emotion. "I've never missed a day since I opened the diner. I've never had to take a sick day or be closed for a holiday. And now that he took my earnings from the last couple days..." she covered her face again and gave into the emotions, letting the tears return.

Matthew stepped forward and pulled her to her feet, folding his arms around her. "You don't have to make any decision right this minute," he said. "Let's just take one thing at a time and talk to the sheriff first."

Jessica nodded and mumbled agreement into his shoulder. It felt so good to be in Matthew's arms, she wished she could just stop time. But, a few minutes later, there was a knock at the door, and their moment was interrupted.

Matthew led the way to the door with Jessica following right behind him.

"Thank you for coming," Matthew said as he opened the door for the sheriff and his deputy.

Jessica agreed. "Yes, thank you both for coming so quickly," she said. "Please come in."

"Well, I'm so sorry to hear this happened to you, Jessica," Sheriff Mark Streen said, sounding sincerely concerned. Mark and his wife visited Heaven's Diner once or twice a week, and they had developed a friendship over time. And Jessica was also starting to get to know the deputy and his family. Little Valley was a small town filled with close friendships. Although there had been some criminal activity in the past few months, Jessica never imagined that she would be a victim. She was so grateful to have people that she knew and trusted, like Mark and Christopher, to be able to take over the case and help her.

"Well, let's get down to business so we can get to the bottom of this. Could you please tell us exactly what you remember, Jessica, from the very beginning," Sheriff Streen began, pulling his small notepad and pen out of his front pocket. Jessica nodded and took a deep breath, exhaling before she began talking. Recounting the experience, she took the Sheriff to the back office to show him the safe and the back door where the robber fled. The deputy took Matthew's account while standing in the front dining room.

"Do you know the amount of money that was in the safe?" The sheriff asked Jessica, as they stood looking at the open safe.

"I have it written in my books. It's the cash I made over the past two days," Jessica responded, a pit forming in her stomach. "But it was more than that, Mark," Jessica said.

"More than the cash?"

"Yes. I also had a diamond ring in there. He took that, too. It was wrapped in that small piece of cloth there," Jessica said, pointing to the swatch of emerald green fabric on the floor peeking out from under her desk.

"It was my mother's engagement ring," she said quietly, her face turned down. "And that was a piece of my mother's favorite dress."

Mark reached out and touched Jessica's arm tenderly. "I'm so sorry, Jessica. You didn't deserve this."

"Thank you," Jessica said. She looked up with hope in her eyes. "Do you think that you might be able to get the ring back?"

"I am going to do everything I can to get everything back to you, Jessica," Mark said reassuringly.

The deputy walked into the storage room with what looked like a small toolbox. "I grabbed any fingerprints I could off the front door, Sheriff. Ready to see what I can get back here now," he said, asking for permission to interrupt.

"Great," the sheriff nodded. "Jessica says he reached into the safe here, and it's a long shot, but we might get something off this piece of fabric that he touched here." Mark pointed out the piece of velvet on the floor to Deputy Jones.

"Well, it's good that the guy wasn't wearing gloves. It would be great if we can match up fingerprints because there isn't much else to go on here. No one else saw anything, I'm afraid," the deputy chimed in.

"Oh, my gosh, I just remembered something!" Jessica grabbed the sheriff's right wrist. "When the guy reached into the safe, I saw a tattoo on his arm, here." She turned the sheriff's wrist over and pointed to the area on his wrist just above his palm.

The sheriff's eyes brightened. "Great! What do you remember about the tattoo?" he asked eagerly.

"It was a bird. It was all black and its wings were open, as if it were flying," she recalled. Her voice was filled with excitement.

The sheriff wrote the description in his notepad, nodding. "Very good, Jessica," he said as he ushered her out of the small office making room for the deputy to collect whatever evidence he needed.

"Is there anything else? I know he was wearing a mask and you gave me height and build, but is there anything he said or did that struck you as odd or familiar?"

"Familiar?" Jessica repeated. *Could she personally know this person?* She shook her head. *There's no way,* she thought. "No, I can't think of anything," she told the sheriff. She suddenly felt tired and wanted a break from all of this.

The sheriff seemed to notice her shift in energy and said, "It's ok. Sometimes more memories or thoughts will come to mind after a while. I know this was very traumatizing for you and that there is a very real feeling of violation that comes along with being robbed. We're almost done here, and we'll get started hunting this guy down right away. But you know where to find me if you remember anything else."

Jessica nodded. "Thank you so much, Mark. I really appreciate that." She paused before continuing, "So, then if I'm done here, I'm going to go clean up and see what I need to do to get my day started."

Mark confirmed that they would be finished in just a few minutes, and Jessica headed to the small public restroom between the storage room and the dining room. She splashed cold water on her face and stared into her reflection in the mirror as she patted her face dry with paper towels. Keeping eye contact with herself, she leaned forward, propping her hands on the edge of the sink. She took a deep breath and exhaled slowly, repeating until she felt a bit calmer. And stronger. She stood tall, pushed her shoulders back and ran her fingers through her long naturally wavy hair.

"Everything is ok," Jessica said quietly to her reflection. And then she repeated it a few more times hoping she could convince herself. She knew she needed to open the diner, and it was going to take every bit of courage and strength she could muster to make it through the day as if everything were normal.

She pushed open the bathroom door and stepped into the dining room. She gasped for a second time that day, before a smile spread across her face.

"Oh, my gosh, what are you two doing here?" She asked the twin sisters, standing behind the counter with aprons on over their plain dresses.

Beth began placing platters of fresh cinnamon rolls into the pastry case. Anna was wringing out a wet cloth over the sink. She folded the cloth in two and set it down on the counter before walking over to Jessica and giving her a warm hug.

"Matthew told us about what happened to you this morning, Jessica. Beth and I are here to help," she said with a smile.

Jessica hugged Anna tightly and ran over to squeeze Beth next. "Oh, my gosh, thank you so much! Do you have time to help, though? I know you must be so busy!"

Beth turned back to filling the pastry case. "Nonsense. Nothing is more important than helping you right now. We have a proverb that says, 'A friend is like...'"

Anna chimed in and the sisters finished the proverb in unison, "...a rainbow. Always there for you after a storm."

The three women laughed, and Jessica's heart overflowed. She looked out the front window and saw Matthew standing in front of his shop across the street. She ran to the window and waved to say thank you. He tipped his hat and smiled that wonderful warm smile that she had grown to love.

Chapter Six

Beth flipped the sign on the front door of Heaven's Diner to read "Open" just minutes after saying goodbye to Sheriff Streen and Deputy Jones. She turned and clasped her hands together.

"We're open!" She squealed with excitement.

Anna chimed in, "Okay, I think we're ready!"

Jessica looked up from the counter where she was sanitizing laminated menus. She chuckled at the sisters' excitement.

Beth approached Jessica. "Why don't you let me do that?" she asked, gently taking the cleaning cloth from her.

Anna agreed. "Jessica, you've shown us how to run the register, and we've gone over all the specials. If you're comfortable with me and Beth running the shop after you've seen how we handle the breakfast rush, you should take the rest of the day off and recuperate."

Jessica sighed. "That's so generous of you both, but I can't expect you to do that for me…"

"Why not?" Beth asked kindly. "Please consider it. You've been through a lot, and you should take care of yourself. Your customers depend on you and the diner." She smiled warmly.

Jessica looked relieved as she agreed to consider it.

The bell on the front door jingled as the first customers entered the diner.

"Welcome to Heaven's Diner!" Anna called out first. "Go ahead and find a seat," she said, her voice full of excitement. Anna and Beth had helped their cousin, Eva Zook, manage her bakery before, and they both thoroughly enjoyed another opportunity to work in a restaurant setting.

The guests chose a booth by the window, and Anna ran over to greet them with menus and glasses of cold water. Jessica watched from behind the counter. Her energy was zapped, and she looked as if she were lost in thought.

Beth expected Jessica would be distracted. She truly hoped that Jessica would take them up on her offer to leave things in their hands.

"Are you okay?" Beth asked her gingerly. Jessica nodded, her eyes clouded.

"I just can't push it out of my mind, you know?" she said.

Beth nodded. "I can only imagine. I'm so glad you weren't hurt, Jessica. We can certainly be grateful for that."

Jessica nodded but remained silent.

Beth directed her by the arm to rest on the stool behind the counter. "You sit. We'll let you know if we have any questions."

Two more families entered the restaurant. Beth worked behind the counter, preparing a serving tray with more glasses of water and menus. Anna set down the empty tray she had and grabbed the new one. She went table to table, greeting the new customers and taking the orders from those that were ready. She brought the orders back to Beth who proceeded to start cooking and plating the requests.

The sisters fell into line, working seamlessly together, without much communication needed. Jessica watched in admiration and with every minute that passed, she was more and more attracted to the offer they had made.

When she caught both sisters in the kitchen area at the same time, Jessica said, "You two are really good at this! I'm so impressed with how quickly you managed to pick everything up!"

Beth and Anna exchanged happy glances. "This is so much fun. We are really enjoying it," Beth said.

Anna nodded. "Although, I am even more impressed that you do all of this by yourself every day, Jessica," she said.

Beth agreed. "*Jah*, that is so true."

Jessica smiled weakly. "Well, I have systems in place, and it helps to have really wonderful, and patient, customers." She said, pausing before continuing. "You know, I think I will take you up on the offer to go get some rest. It feels weird leaving here, but I will just need a few hours to feel better. I'll be back before dinner, if that's still okay."

Beth grinned, "Of course, it's okay! Go, go! We'll be fine!" She waved her hand in the air as if to shoo her out the door.

Anna nodded, "Yes, Jessica. Let us do this for you. Take whatever time you need."

Jessica thanked the sisters again and gathered her purse, before heading out the front door.

Anna turned to Beth and asked, "Are you doing *gut* back here?"

"Yep," Beth said with a grin. "What about you?" She knew that Anna offered to handle the tables to help accommodate for Beth's social anxiety.

"I'm doing fine," Anna said. "This is fun!"

The two worked together to get through the breakfast rush, and as the restaurant cleared out, they took a quick break behind the front counter with fresh cups of coffee. Their chat about their morning was interrupted by another sound of the bell on the front door. The sisters looked up to find an attractive man they did not recognize entering the diner. He looked out of place in Little Valley, dressed in perfectly pressed dark slacks and a crisp light-blue cotton dress shirt, buttoned almost all the way to his neck.

A look mixed with surprise and confusion crossed his face when he set eyes on the two women. They sat behind the counter, identical, dressed in plain dresses. Their hair was pulled into neat buns with *kapps* pinned on top. He stopped in mid-stride, in the center of the empty diner.

"Welcome to Heaven's Diner!" Anna called out. "Go ahead and take a seat wherever you'd like."

The man approached the counter. "Thank you, ma'am," he greeted them. "Is Jessica McLean here?" He asked, one eyebrow slightly raised.

The sisters glanced at each other before answering.

"No, she is not here right now. Can I help you?" Anna asked politely. "Would you like to have a seat?"

The man hesitated for a moment. Then, as he settled onto a stool at the counter, he said, "Sure. Thank you."

He reached out his hand to Anna and said, "My name is James. James McLean. I'm Jessica's ex-husband."

Beth took in a quick breath but tried to hide the shock on her face.

Anna hesitated but handed him a menu and politely shook his hand. "I'm Anna Miller, and this is my sister, Beth Troyer," Anna said.

"It's a pleasure to meet you both," James said, extending an invite to shake hands to Beth next. She politely declined with a small wave and a nod of her head.

"Can I pour you a cup of coffee?" Beth asked the man, rising to her feet and reaching for a clean coffee cup from the shelf.

"That sounds wonderful," James said. He glanced at the fancy watch on his left wrist and nonchalantly asked, "So, when do you expect Jessica to return?"

Anna and Beth glanced at each other as Beth set the steaming hot cup of coffee on the counter in front of him. Both women began talking at the same time.

"We're not sure…," Beth began.

"Sometime later…," Anna said.

James chuckled before taking a sip. "Got it," he said.

A feeling of uneasiness was starting to form in Beth's gut. "I mean, we'd be happy to pass along a message for her, if you'd like," she said, straining to keep her voice light.

James set his cup back down on the counter, "No message," he said as he looked from one sister to the other. "I was just coming by to say hi. I came by the other day to see her for the first time in a while, and it was just so good to catch up. So, I thought I'd make the trip out here again today."

"Oh? Where are you from?" Anna asked politely, staying busy wrapping silverware behind the counter.

"I'm from a town called Billingsley, about sixty miles north of here. That's where Jessica and I lived for the length of our marriage. Have you ever been there?" His tone was cordial.

Beth shook her head, "No, I don't think we have. We sure love having Jessica here, though. She's like part of the family to us."

James smiled, "Yeah, everyone loves Jess. She's an easy person to love." He finished his coffee and set his cup down, wiping his mouth with the paper napkin from the dispenser on the counter. He folded it neatly and lifted his cup, carefully setting the cup on the napkin. "Well, it's been real nice meeting the two of you. Jess is lucky to have such good help in the shop."

The sisters remained silent, both keeping busy with their hands. Anna rolling silverware and Beth rearranging the pastries in the case. They ignored the reference to the two of them being Jessica's "help." Beth wanted to give him the benefit of the doubt that he might not have meant it that way, but she still couldn't shake that uneasy feeling.

"Maybe I'll just swing by Jess's house to see her before I head back home," he said. "She's out on McVay Road, right?"

Beth's suspicions grew. She and Anna had grown up in Little Valley, and they both knew there was no McVay Road in town. It was clear he was trying to ask for Jessica's address.

Anna must have been thinking the same thing because she quickly responded, "I'm not sure of Jessica's address, actually."

Beth chimed in with a small laugh, "*Jah*, she pretty much lives here at the diner."

"Ha, that's right," Anna said, joining in with her sister. "She does."

Then turning back toward James, she said, "We'll let her know you came by. It was good to meet you."

"Thank you kindly," he said. Beth thought the man was trying to turn on his charm, but there was something about him she couldn't trust.

Pulling a five-dollar bill out of his wallet, he dropped it on the counter and said, "Please do tell Jess I said hello and that I'll see her next time."

He stood to leave. "You ladies have a good day now," he said in the same charming tone.

The ladies exchanged goodbyes with James and wished him a wonderful day. After the door closed behind him, Beth turned to Anna. "I don't know what to think of that guy," she said.

Anna looked at Beth and said, "Now, let's not jump to conclusions. We'll tell Jessica he came by. It's possible that they're still friends, so we don't want to think the worst."

Beth nodded in agreement. "You're right. No jumping to conclusions, but you and I both know there is no such thing as a McVay Road in Little Valley."

"Well, I can't argue that," Anna said. "But there's no harm done. We should get busy."

Beth agreed, and the sisters pushed their thoughts aside and set their focus on prepping for the lunch crowd.

Chapter Seven

Matthew stood on the bishop's front porch. He said a quick prayer to set good intentions for his check-in meeting before knocking on the door. He was nervous to ask the bishop for more time before scheduling his baptism, but he just couldn't commit until he saw the direction his relationship with Jessica was headed. And for that, he needed more time.

A small-framed woman opened the big heavy door. Her silver-gray hair was tucked into her *kapp*, and long lavender colored dress hung on her body like heavy curtains.

"*Gut daag*," Margaret Packer greeted Matthew. The bishop's wife had kind eyes and a soft-spoken voice. She was just past fifty years old, but she easily looked like she was approaching sixty-five. Her face was pale and showed sadness, even with a smile. Her body appeared frail and weak with slumped shoulders and bad posture. Matthew remembered the terrible time only months earlier when the bishop's youngest daughter was kidnapped, and he could tell the trauma had taken a toll on the girl's mother.

"*Wie bischt*, Mrs. Packer?" Matthew asked, politely.

"I'm fine, *denki,*" Margaret responded, forcing a smile. "Come in, please. Bishop Packer is expecting you." She led Matthew to the small office just off the living room. The bishop sat at his desk, his eyes closed in prayer. His hand hovered over a notebook, lightly gripping a pencil.

Margaret and Matthew entered the room, but both stood together quietly as the bishop finished his prayer. Their eyes were fixed on the floor, and their hands folded in front of them. After a few moments, the bishop opened his eyes and cleared his throat.

"Ah, *gut daag*, Matthew!" He greeted Matthew joyously, rising to his feet. He shook Matthew's hand and patted him on the back. Turning to Margaret, both men thanked her, and she nodded, pulling the door shut behind her.

"*Wilkumme*," the bishop said to Matthew, "please, have a seat."

"*Denki*," Matthew said, relaxing into the upholstered chair facing the desk. He was already feeling a bit more at ease.

"It is such a beautiful day today," Bishop Packer spoke as he gestured out the large window next to his desk. He settled into his leather office chair, facing Matthew. "It's almost a shame to be inside."

Matthew chuckled, "Ah, yes, it is a bit chilly, though. I love the signs of Autumn with the leaves changing color and drifting to the ground, but I must admit I already miss the warmer weather."

"*Jah*, I know what you mean. But we are approaching the holidays, which is always *gut*."

Matthew nodded.

The bishop changed the subject. "So, tell me. How have you been?" He asked curiously.

Matthew paused before responding. "I've been very *gut*, *denki*," he said.

"Well, as you know, we are meeting today to check on where things are with you and your commitment to the faith," the bishop spoke in a matter-of-fact tone.

Matthew nodded but did not yet respond.

"Have you been studying?" The bishop continued.

"*Jah*," Matthew said pensively. "I have been studying."

The bishop sat silent, waiting for Matthew to continue.

"Bishop Packer, as you know, during Rumspringa, I strayed from the faith. I had fallen in love with a woman who chose my best friend as her life-long partner instead of me. Looking back, I know that part of what happened to pull me away was my pride, but after much introspection, I can admit that I also questioned the Lord's choices. I searched for why I was not selected to be the one who would live happily ever after with this *gut* woman. I was overcome with emotions. I was confused. Sad. And I was also a bit angry, if I'm honest." Matthew removed his hat and laid it on his lap. He ran his fingers through his hair.

"As a result, I lived many years as a lonely man. I never found anyone that touched my heart in the same way that she did. I asked *Gotte* over and over again when would it be my turn. When would my suffering end?" Matthew paused.

The bishop sat silently, leaning back in his chair slightly, his hands clasped together in his lap. He nodded for Matthew to continue.

"I spent many hours praying, and after some time, I finally resolved my anger with *Gotte*. I learned to trust him and follow the path that he wants me to follow." Matthew fidgeted in his seat.

"And then, I heard about Moses Schrock and his arrest. My childhood friend, who at one time felt so much like my own *bruder*, needed my support. I instantly felt *Gotte's* calling to return to the community." Matthew paused as he remembered.

"The message was so clear that I didn't even give it a second thought. I was nervous, *jah*, not sure how I would be received by Moses or his wife. Or the rest of the community. But I felt confident that the Lord would be by my side."

The bishop nodded. "*Jah*, it was *gut* of you to listen to *Gotte* and return."

Matthew smiled. "And it has been *wunderbaar*. More than I ever expected. Everyone was so welcoming. There has never been any tension, and I have grown very close to the Schrock family since my return. I believe I have also proven that I want to contribute to the community, both financially and emotionally. It is very important to me that I carry my load and have something to offer to the *wunderbaar* people and families here."

The bishop smiled, "*Jah*. Your contribution has not gone unnoticed."

Matthew nodded and continued, "*Denki*. It truly feels like home again. The things I contribute come effortlessly."

The bishop then asked the question that Matthew knew was the real reason he was there. "So, you sound like you are ready to commit, Matthew. But Minister Brandenburger mentioned that your baptism has not yet been scheduled." He posed the last sentence as if it were a question. "I am assuming this has something to do with your relationship with Ms. McLean?"

Matthew took a deep breath and adjusted his posture, pulling his shoulders back. After a moment, he nodded. "That is correct, Bishop," he said matter-of-factly.

The bishop remained still, again waiting for Matthew to continue his thoughts.

"Like I said, I believe that coming back to Little Valley was *Gotte's* plan for me," Matthew found himself feeling more and more nervous as he approached the topic of Jessica. "And I also believe that plan may include Ms. McLean."

The bishop nodded. "You mentioned that, *jah*. But there are complications," the bishop paused, "as we spoke about previously."

Matthew nodded and carefully interjected, "*Jah*, and that's what I'm saying, I guess. I can't commit to getting baptized until I know for sure if I am supposed to be with Jessica or not." There, he said it. Matthew let out a breath and deflated back into his seat, waiting for the bishop's response.

The bishop sat and stroked his beard. "Hmm. Well, what is your plan then, Matthew? When will you know if you want to pursue a life with Jessica outside of the Amish faith or not?"

Matthew sighed. "Honestly, Bishop, I don't want to choose."

The bishop chuckled briefly before saying, "I understand that it is difficult when faced with two paths. But I will remind you that you can only begin a journey by first deciding on a destination. You must first know what you want."

"But that's what I'm saying. I want both. I want to pursue a relationship with Jessica *and* be a part of this community. How can I have that, Bishop?" Matthew pleaded, leaning forward in his seat.

"I'm afraid you know the answer to this, Matthew. In our faith, dating involves joining together in church service and gathering at community events. It is not acceptable for an Amish gentleman to marry an *Englischer*."

Matthew nodded.

"I still stand in my position that if you are going to pursue a godly relationship with Ms. McLean, you cannot do this as a baptized man. If that is standing in your way of becoming baptized, then you are not yet fully committed, and I wouldn't be able to approve the baptism."

Matthew hung his head.

The bishop sat up straighter in his chair. "*Sohn*, if *Gotte* has sent you down this path, there will be more clarity along the way. It is your responsibility to be open to seeing what you are being shown. I worry about your heart deceiving you and leading you astray again, but I am praying for you to find the answers, and the happiness, you seek."

Matthew looked at the bishop with gratitude in his eyes, but before he could speak, the bishop held up his hand and continued.

"You must know, however, that your decision will be forced soon. There are men in the community who are doubting your intentions and outwardly expressing their concerns to each other. I'm afraid that you must be prepared to face discontent at some point. It will not be easy, but it is very important that you remember to abide by the rules of the *Ordnung* and show respect as long as you are living among us. Whether you are baptized yet or not."

Matthew was quiet, but he nodded his head. "I understand, Bishop. And I can appreciate what you must be having to explain to other members on my behalf. Trust that I will make this important decision very soon, and whichever road I choose to follow, I will always be grateful for your kindness and guidance."

The bishop stood and walked to the door. With his hand on the knob, he turned back and said, "Pray often, Matthew. Listen to *Gotte*" he paused, "but keep in mind that nothing is black and white."

Chapter Eight

Anna and Beth stood in line waiting patiently to place their order at their cousin's bakery, Sugar on Top. Eva Zook caught a glimpse of the identical sisters standing there and waved them over.

"Y'all don't have to stand in line," she said, giving each of the sisters a hug hello. "It's so good to see you! It feels like it has been forever. Thanks for coming by!"

"Of course! It has been a few weeks. You are so busy all the time with the success of this place," Anna said gesturing toward the line.

"We're meeting Abigail and Jonah here. Will you have time to sit with us for a few minutes, at least, do you think?" Beth asked. She missed seeing Eva at her home every day, but she was so proud of how quickly the people in Little Valley took to the bakery and how well Eva was doing with keeping up with all of it.

"I'll try, but we're just hitting our afternoon rush. There's something about coffee and a snack at three o'clock that drives everyone in here," Eva beamed.

"Well, you must come over for Sunday dinner, then," Anna said. "It just hasn't been the same since you moved into your own place, but we want to hear all about it."

"That's a promise," Eva said. "I can do Sunday dinner."

Beth and Anna grinned.

"So, what can I get for you ladies? Go ahead and have a seat and I'll bring it out to you," Eva said.

Beth spoke up first, "We'll just have four black coffees and whatever snack you recommend. We're easy." She winked at Eva.

"Coming up!" Eva said, and the sisters headed over to a cozy table for four off to the right.

Just as they removed their shawls and got settled, they saw Abigail and Jonah walk in the front door together.

"Wow, they came together today," Beth said to Anna. Anna raised her eyebrows.

Beth waved her daughter and son over to their table, and both she and her sister jumped up to hug each of them before they all sat down together.

"I'm so glad to see you both!" Beth squealed. "Eva's bringing coffee and snacks in a minute."

"This place is packed," Jonah said. "You know, I think this is my first time here."

Abigail turned to look at her younger brother with an exaggerated shocked expression. "What? That's crazy, Jonah! Where have you been?"

Jonah laughed and rolled his eyes. "I'm always at work, I guess," he said.

"How *is* work at the inn?" Anna asked. "Are you still liking it?"

"Well, things have changed quite a bit in the past few months, and I don't know..." Jonah's voice trailed off.

"What do you mean?" Beth asked. "Do you not still like working there?"

"Well, it's just not my passion, you know? I think I'm getting bored," Jonah explained.

Abigail piped up, "What is your passion, little *bruder*?"

Jonah shrugged. "I guess I haven't really found it yet."

Beth rolled her eyes. "All this talk about passion. Do you think your *dat* chose to apprentice his *dat* because he was passionate about carpentry? No. He did it because his father offered to teach him how to do it. At first, he didn't enjoy the craft, but as he learned and developed his skills, he began to love the work."

Abigail and Noah listened respectfully to their mother although this was not their first time hearing this speech.

"And *that* is how passion is developed. It doesn't just fall from the sky. You are not born to be a woodworker or a farmer. You take the opportunities. You build your skills. And you become dedicated to your craft. Passion will show up with experience." Beth finished just as Eva showed up with a tray of four coffee cups, cream and sugar, four servings of plates, napkins and silverware, and a beautiful raspberry tea ring. She set everything on the table and after warmly greeting Abigail and Jonah, she promised to be back soon to check on things.

The conversation shifted as the four of them added their cream and sugar to their coffee and shared the tea ring. Abigail asked about all her siblings and cousins, and Anna and Beth shared all the family news. Sarah and Moses were thinking about having another baby. Amos was splitting time between helping Eli prepare the farm for winter and working in the Mast produce store. Nothing new was going on with Faith and Peter, but things were fine, and everyone was excited to gather for the upcoming Thanksgiving holiday.

"Did Matthew ever set a date for his baptism?" Jonah asked between bites.

Anna and Beth glanced at each other.

"I'm not sure," Beth said. "I haven't heard anything."

Anna shrugged her shoulders. "Me either," she said.

"Is he dating Ms. McLean from Heaven's Diner, though?" Abigail asked.

Beth and Anna shrugged in unison this time.

"Poor Jessica was robbed yesterday morning. I'm not sure if you two heard about that," Beth said nonchalantly.

Abigail gasped. "No, I didn't," she said, setting her fork down. "Is she okay?"

Jonah looked up from his plate. "Did they catch the guy?" he asked.

Anna shook her head. "Not yet," she said. "At least not that we know of."

"Jessica is fine," Beth said, and then continued with sheepish excitement. "And your Aunt Anna and I ran the diner for her yesterday, so she could recuperate."

Anna nodded, "She was pretty shook up."

"We had a *wunderbaar* time cooking and serving the customers," Beth continued.

"Well, I'm so glad she isn't hurt," Abigail said. "That is so scary."

Jonah agreed, "*Jah.* Now that I work at the inn, I see so many strangers coming through Little Valley." He swallowed a gulp of coffee and continued, "Most of them are nice, but some are just... well,... strange."

"What do you mean?" Beth asked, her tone laden with worry. Anna squeezed her hand under the table. Beth knew Anna didn't want her to jump to conclusions.

"Some are just not friendly, you know. Most of the people who come to the inn are nice and respectful, but then I feel like some of them are just drifters and are actually surprised that it's an *Amish* inn when they show up. But they book a room anyway." Jonah took another gulp.

Beth looked concerned. "Are they mean to you? Are you in any kind of danger?"

Jonah rolled his eyes. "*Maem*, it's ok. It's not like that. Relax. I'm fine."

Abigail interjected before Beth could respond. "So, I guess now is as good a time as any to share my news, then," she said.

If she wanted to distract Beth, it worked. Beth shifted her attention from worrying about Jonah to worrying about Abigail. "What is it, honey?" Beth asked her daughter. Fear was surfacing, and it was showing up as a pit inside her stomach.

Abigail cleared her throat and fidgeted in her seat. "Well," she said, pausing before she continued, "Jeremiah got a really great job offer in a town about sixty miles north from here."

"What?" Beth gasped. She felt like the walls were closing in, and she was starting to panic. She squeezed Anna's hand under the table and held tight.

"That's *wunderbaar* news, Abigail," Jonah said, setting down his cup. "Please tell Jeremiah I said congratulations."

Beth sat speechless.

"Tell us more. What job is it? When? Is Jeremiah excited?" Anna said, turning to clasp Beth's hand with her other hand, as well.

Abigail beamed. "It's a very successful leathersmith shop. It has been a family business for over fifty years, but the owner is retiring. His son has decided to go to college and pursue law instead of staying in the business. So, the family is looking for help. They have been visiting different leathersmith shops, and Jeremiah's little shop was one of them. They were so impressed with his work that they asked him if he would be open to a management position."

Beth could see the excitement in her daughter's face, and she wanted to be happy for her. But she had feared her children moving away, and now she was having to face that fear head on. She pushed back tears and forced a smile on her face as Abigail continued.

"They offered him a salary that is more than three times what he has ever made with his own shop here, and he really likes the family."

"Is the family Amish?" Beth managed to ask.

Abigail shook her head and took a sip of her coffee. "Well, no, they're not. But there is an Amish community nearby. Just in the next small town over. That is where we will settle down. Jeremiah has already met them, and they are excited for an addition to their community."

"You've already decided for sure you're going, then?" Beth asked. She tried desperately to hide her feelings, but she knew that Abigail could see that she was upset.

Abigail reached over and touched her arm. "*Jah, Maem*. We have decided," she said softly.

The mood at the table had shifted.

"We're going to miss you, *Schwester*," Jonah said, wrapping his arm around his sister's shoulders. "But we're happy for you and Jeremiah."

Anna nodded, "*Jah*, we are sad to see you go, of course, but we trust that it is *Gotte's* calling for you and Jeremiah. And because of that, we will celebrate. Right, *Schwester*?" She looked at Beth and squeezed her hand.

Beth sat up straight and nodded. "*Jah*, that is right. We will help you move and get settled. We would love to meet the community, of course. And if you're only sixty miles away, we can visit often." Beth was feeling a bit stronger about it all, commenting on how proud she was of Jeremiah and how brave Abigail was to take on this new adventure.

Anna agreed, nodding emphatically. "So, you never did tell us where you were going?" She asked, as Beth took a sip of coffee.

74

"Oh, the leathersmith shop is in a town called Billingsley," she said. "Have you ever heard of it?"

Beth almost choked on her mouthful of coffee. She and Anna looked at each other, thinking the same thoughts without an exchange of words: *What an eerie coincidence.*

Beth squeezed Anna's hand again. The pit in her stomach was back.

Chapter Nine

Jessica parked in front of Heaven's Diner. It was the same time she arrived every other morning, but she had been on edge since the masked man had accosted her at this time just three days earlier. She pulled the purse strap over her head and took a deep breath. She reached for the car door handle to open the driver's side door when there was a soft knock on her window. She let out a scream that was cut short as soon as she saw that it was Matthew Beiler.

He put his hands up and said, "Oh, my gosh, I'm so sorry. I'm so sorry," as she opened the door.

She giggled and grabbed his hands. "It's ok. I'm just jumpy," she assured him. "I'm glad it is you."

A large smile spread across his face. "Whew! I'm sure glad you didn't faint or anything," he laughed.

"Me, too!" She grinned. Then, realizing it was much earlier than normal for Matthew to be opening his shop, she asked, "What are you doing here, anyway? Besides trying to scare me to death?" She teased him, poking his arm with her gloved finger.

Matthew grinned and shrugged, "I just couldn't sleep, so I thought I'd keep you company while you opened shop today." The truth was that he had secretly been watching Jessica in the early mornings for the past two days, arriving early at his shop to watch from across the street and make sure she got inside safely. But he was running late today and arrived just after she had. He decided to see if she was open to him walking her in.

"Well, thank you. I appreciate that. A lot. I was actually going to ask you if you wouldn't mind meeting me here early for a few days until I felt a little better, but I thought it might be an imposition." She pulled her hat down further onto her head and rubbed her gloved hands together.

"Ah, I wish you had asked!" Matthew said. "It's no imposition at all."

"You're the best, Matthew," Jessica smiled. She locked the car door and turned to walk towards the front door.

Matthew put his hand on the small of her back and she instantly felt safer.

This time, she held the key to the door in her hand, ready to insert it in the slot and get inside quickly. She went to slip the key in the lock, but the door moved.

"That's weird," she said. "It's open."

"What? Wait..." but before Matthew could say anything else, Jessica had pushed the door open and stepped inside. She flipped on the light switch on the right and screamed. Her keys fell to the floor as she turned and fell into Matthew's arms.

"*Ach du lieva*!" Matthew exclaimed, his arms tightened around Jessica. "This is not good."

Just a couple feet away from where Matthew and Jessica stood was a man, laying face down in a puddle of blood.

Jessica's face was buried in Matthew's shoulder. "Is he dead?" she asked, her voice muffled.

"Um," Matthew said, "I don't know." His voice turned to a whisper, "Jessica, we need to get out of here. We don't know if the guy who did this is still here."

He began taking slow, deliberate steps back out of the door, pulling him along with her.

She lifted her head and snapped out of it, though, "Oh my gosh, Matthew," was all she could muster to say.

He grabbed her hand and led her across the street to his flower shop. They ran alongside the side of the building to the back, looking around cautiously. He fished the keys out of his coat pocket and unlocked the back door. They stepped inside and locked the heavy door behind them. He flipped on the lights and the two of them stared at each other.

"Okay," Matthew said, his breathing was rushed and heavy.

Jessica stood with her gloved hands over her mouth. "What are we going to do, Matthew? Who was that? And why would someone kill somebody in my diner?" Tears started to roll down her face as everything that they just witnessed started to soak in.

"It's okay," Matthew said. He pulled a chair out of the storage room and guided Jessica to sit down. "We should call the sheriff," he said.

Jessica nodded, wiping the tears with the back of her gloves.

Matthew stretched through the storage room doorway to look out the front window.

"Do you see anything?" Jessica asked.

Matthew shook his head. "Nothing looks any different. The door closed behind us, and there's no one out there," he said.

Jessica let out a sigh of relief. "Okay, let's call the sheriff, then. Do you have a phone here?" She knew the Amish didn't typically have telephones.

"Yes, for the business," Matthew said. "Now that I think about it, though, the sheriff won't be in yet. And I think it's best we just call 911. I'll do that now. You stay here where it's safe."

Jessica nodded and pulled her coat tighter around her. "Yes, that's a good idea," she said.

Matthew stepped into the front of his small store, and Jessica listened as he made the phone call.

"Hi, yes, we need an ambulance at Heaven's Diner on Main Street in Little Valley," he said. "Um, it looks like a man was... well, a man is lying on the ground and there's a lot of blood..." he stammered.

"The owner, Jessica McLean is here with me. I was helping her.. I mean, she was opening her shop when... We were both there when we found him." Matthew sounded scared and bewildered.

Jessica wondered if she should intervene but decided against it and stayed seated, listening carefully.

"My name? My name is Matthew Beiler. I'm the owner of the shop across the street." The dispatcher had started asking questions, and Matthew sounded even more nervous than before.

"The Secret Garden," he said, sounding a bit ruffled. "The name of my shop is The Secret Garden. The man that needs an ambulance is across the street at Heaven's Diner." He paused as the dispatcher continued.

"No, ma'am, we don't know. No, we didn't check his pulse, ma'am."

Jessica sat there, fidgeting in her seat. *Who could've done this?* she thought to herself. *And who was that, and why was he in her diner?*

"No, we didn't see anyone. We left and came over here because we didn't know if the person could still be there." Matthew continued explaining everything to the dispatcher.

"Thank you. Could you also please let Sheriff Streen know? Yes, Sheriff Mark Streen from Mainstay County. Yes, that is correct." It sounded to Jessica like the phone call was coming to an end.

"Will the ambulance be here soon, ma'am?" Matthew asked politely.

As if on cue, Jessica heard sirens faintly, the sound growing louder as the ambulance, fire truck and police car moved in closer.

"Yes, they are here," Matthew said. "Thank you very much for your help." He hung up the phone and walked back around the corner to Jessica.

She was on her feet. "Thank you, Matthew. I guess we should go out there when they get here," she said.

Matthew nodded. Jessica thought he looked worried.

"Hopefully that guy will be okay, and everything will be solved quickly," Jessica said.

"Right. Would you mind if I pray for a minute?" Matthew asked softly.

"No, of course not," Jessica said. She walked toward him, and as he knelt on the floor, she knelt beside him.

Matthew recited prayers quietly, just under his breath, as Jessica closed her eyes and remained silent. She had not been raised with any type of spiritual background, so she wasn't sure she even knew how to pray. But she desperately wanted to learn. She had envied those that took comfort in prayer and felt in her heart as if something was missing. She squeezed her eyes shut and decided at that moment just to let her thoughts flow and form into prayers of her own.

Dear God, she thought, *please keep us safe from evil. Please let that man in the diner be okay. Please give me back the life I had last week when there was only happiness, and my world wasn't filled with fear.*

She felt Matthew standing, so she quickly and quietly said "*Amen*" before standing to her feet as well.

The sirens were much louder now. Matthew and Jessica rushed to the front of the store. Standing side by side at the window, the two watched in silence as the emergency vehicles parked. And they continued to watch silently as the first responders all jumped out of their vehicles and went into action.

Matthew held Jessica's hand and Jessica's heart raced as they touched. She squeezed his hand, and after a few seconds of just standing there together, Matthew led Jessica out the front door of The Secret Garden and into the street to face whatever lay ahead of them.

Chapter Ten

A police officer walked toward Jessica and Matthew as they headed across the street towards the diner.

"Are you the one that called 911?" The man directed the question toward Matthew. He was a middle-aged man, average build, with short salt and pepper hair peeking out from under his uniform cap.

Matthew nodded and reached out his hand. "Yes, Officer. I'm Matthew Beiler. I own the flower shop," he said as he gestured toward The Secret Garden. "And this is Jessica McLean. She owns Heaven's Diner," he explained.

The officer shook Matthew's hand and then reached out for Jessica's. "Nice to meet you both," he said. "So, any idea what happened here?"

"We were about to ask you the same thing," Jessica said. "We found the man laying there on my floor when we opened the door to the diner just about twenty or thirty minutes ago."

The officer cocked his head and looked back at Matthew. "So, y'all were together when you found the body?"

Matthew and Jessica nodded. "That's right," Matthew said.

"Do you normally open the shop with Ms. McLean, Mr. Beiler?" The cop's question sounded a bit too accusatory for Jessica's taste.

She interjected, "No, of course not. Matthew was helping me out this morning," she said. "I was robbed a few days ago. In the morning. When I went to open the shop."

The officer's forehead wrinkled, and his eyes squinted. "Oh, I didn't know that. That's interesting," he said. "Did y'all call the police when you were robbed?" He asked, again, looking at Matthew.

Matthew nodded and fidgeted with his hat.

"Yes, I did," Jessica said, trying to pull the officer's attention back to her. "I called Sheriff Streen. And he and Deputy Jones came out and did the investigation."

The officer smiled, "Ah, you called Sheriff Streen."

Jessica interrupted. "Is the man on the floor in my diner alive, Officer?" she asked. She hoped that the answer would be yes. She can't imagine someone being killed in her diner.

The officer shook his head, "Oh, no, I'm afraid not," he said. "That guy's dead as a doornail."

Jessica lowered her eyes and shook her head.

"Did you know him?" the officer asked.

She looked back at the officer and shrugged, "I don't even know. He was laying face down on the floor, and I didn't get a good look at him."

The officer nodded. "Well, we'll make sure you get to try and identify him then. That will be important, of course."

Jessica's mouth opened but no words came out. She wasn't sure if he meant she would have to look at a dead body or just a picture of the guy, and she was too scared of the answer to ask the question.

Matthew spoke up, "Do you know if Sheriff Streen was contacted?"

The officer shrugged. "I don't know, but I can check. Hang tight over there by my car, will ya? And I'll go find out." He gestured to his police car parked at the back of the pack and turned to walk away.

Matthew gently guided Jessica by the small of her back to the officer's car to wait.

"I really hope Mark gets here soon," Jessica said, looking at her wristwatch.

Matthew nodded. "Me, too. That officer didn't seem too friendly."

Jessica worried for Matthew. She knew what the Amish community had gone through this year with false accusations, and she feared the same could happen to Matthew.

Only moments later, Jessica caught a glimpse of a familiar car heading their way. "It's Mark and Christopher," she said as she grabbed Matthew's arm. She watched as the car parked close by and a wave of relief passed over Matthew's face.

The sheriff and deputy walked over to greet Jessica and Matthew.

"Morning, folks. Looks like we're late to the party," he said as he shook Matthew's hand and tenderly touched Jessica's shoulder. "How are they treating y'all?"

"Fine. We've only talked to one officer, and he told us to wait here until he could figure out if you were on your way or not," Matthew said.

"Well, let me go introduce myself and get the rundown. We'll see if we can't get these people out of your way" the sheriff said as he gestured for the deputy to join him. The two men walked up to the nearest officer, exchanged a few words, and then disappeared into the diner.

"Are you cold?" Matthew asked. "I can ask if we can wait inside my shop, if you'd be more comfortable there."

"That might be a good idea," Jessica said. She wondered if he didn't want all the other shop owners and townspeople to start showing up and see the two of them standing in the street together.

"Hang tight," Matthew said, as he ran off to ask permission.

Jessica stood there, shivering. She wasn't sure if it was because of the cold or if she was in shock. Now that she was alone, she was flooded with thoughts. Unanswered questions swam through her mind. What could've happened? Could this have anything to do with her? Was the person on the floor someone she knew? Was it supposed to be her dead on the floor instead, or was this a message of some kind? She was lost in her thoughts when Matthew stepped back into her view.

"Ok, let's go. I told them we'd be waiting at my shop," he said, taking her arm and gently escorting her to the front door of his flower shop.

Once inside, he brought the chair she had used earlier around to the front of the shop and set it down in the center of the floor. "Have a seat," he said. "At least it's warmer in here."

He grabbed a step stool and set it down across from her, leaning against it, crossing his arms and rubbing his biceps with his hands to get warm. "I wish I had some coffee to offer you," he said. "Ironically, I always come to see you to get my coffee." He smiled.

Jessica returned a closed-lipped grin.

"Did you go inside just now?" She asked Matthew.

He shook his head, "No. I talked to the officer we met. He was standing outside."

Jessica and Matthew sat together quietly as they waited. A few minutes passed and Matthew stood to his feet.

"Ah, they're leaving," he said.

"They're leaving?" Jessica repeated, jumping to her feet to see.

"Well, not the sheriff, but the ambulance is leaving and so is the fire truck."

Jessica and Matthew watched as the sheriff and deputy exited the diner and walked toward them. Jessica moved closer to the door in anticipation.

Mark and Christopher entered, and Jessica stepped back allowing room for everyone in the small shop. She pummeled them with questions. "What did you find out? Who was it? Do they know who did it? Is the guy gone now?"

Mark held up his hand. "Whoa, whoa," he said. "Slow down, Jessica. Please have a seat so we can chat about this."

She nodded and sat back in the chair. The three men remained standing.

Mark began explaining, "Here's what we know so far. The guy was shot in your dining room, and it doesn't look like it happened very long before you arrived."

Jessica gasped and covered her mouth.

"There is no forced entry in the back and doesn't appear to be forced entry in the front either. The front door was unlocked. The back door was secured." He continued, his voice steady.

"Also, the man was shot from inside the diner, not from the doorway. So, evidence shows that someone was standing in the diner near the counter when the man was shot in the head." He paused.

Jessica's mouth hung open, her hands falling limply to her lap. The sheriff squatted down in front of Jessica so that he was more eye level to her before he continued.

"Now, Jessica, I have to tell you that we don't know the guy's name, but he had a tattoo of a bird on his right wrist," the sheriff said slowly.

Jessica's mouth closed.

"What does that mean?" Matthew asked. "What does the tattoo mean?"

Jessica turned to Matthew and said, "The guy that robbed me had a tattoo of a bird on his wrist."

Matthew drew in a quick breath. "Oh, I didn't know that," he said.

Jessica returned her attention to the sheriff. "Do we know who did it, Sheriff? And why did it happen in my diner?"

The sheriff remained squatting and locked his eyes with Jessica's. He shook his head. Slowly, he said, "I need you to tell me exactly what happened this morning. Everything you remember and don't leave any details out, okay?"

Jessica sat silent. She nodded slowly and then recounted how she and Matthew found the man lying on the floor in a puddle of blood.

The sheriff listened as the deputy took notes.

The room fell silent, and the sheriff scratched his unshaven chin. He looked up at the deputy and then looked back at Jessica. "I have to ask you one more question, and then I'm going to help you find someone to come clean the diner for you, okay?" The sheriff almost sounded like he was speaking to a child.

But his voice changed and became more serious with the next question he asked.

"Do you own a gun, Jessica?" He asked pointedly.

Jessica was shocked.

Matthew took a step closer to her.

The deputy and the sheriff waited anxiously to hear her answer. All eyes were on her.

"No, of course I don't own a gun," Jessica said, her voice cracking as she fought back tears. "Why would you ask me that, Mark?" She asked, terrified of the answer.

Mark clasped his hands in front of him. "Because the police officer you met earlier found a handgun hidden under your cash register. And it shoots the same type of bullet that was used in the murder." The sheriff explained slowly.

Jessica felt Matthew's hand rest on her shoulder as a new question joined the others already in her mind. *Surely they don't think I killed this guy?*

The deputy spoke up next. "Did you kill the guy in self-defense, Jessica?" He asked the question politely and with a hint of hope.

Matthew stepped forward. "No!" His voice was angry and stern. "Jessica didn't kill anyone, Deputy." He turned to the sheriff. "She already told you both exactly what happened. And I'm her witness."

The sheriff nodded and straightened his legs, standing tall. "Ok, Matthew, we get it. Trust me, I don't think Jessica did it either, but we have the hard job of having to ask stupid questions sometimes. There must be an explanation. Let us go work on clearing this up with the other officers." Mark turned to Jessica, who sat silently in the chair.

"Jessica, with your permission, I'll handle getting the place cleaned up and hang a closed 'due to emergency' sign on the door for today."

Jessica nodded and whispered, "Thank you, Mark."

Mark reached over and patted her shoulder, "Of course. Now, go home and get some rest. Let's talk more about this tomorrow, what d'ya say?"

Jessica nodded and Matthew walked the men out of the shop. Jessica stood and edged her way to the door, standing unseen against the wall between the door and the window.

She heard Matthew say, "Look, I want to apologize if I got out of line in there, Sheriff, but I just don't believe there's any way Jessica could do that. Not even in self-defense."

The sheriff tipped his hat to Matthew. "I hear what you're saying, Matthew," the sheriff said, "Jessica is my friend, too, but in my line of work, we have to look at everything with a new set of eyes, you understand."

There was a short pause in the conversation and Jessica leaned a little closer to the open door.

"You know what I mean, right?" the sheriff continued, "I guess I'm trying to say that things aren't always what they seem."

Jessica's heart jumped into her throat. She knew she was in trouble, and she needed help.

Chapter Eleven

"Let me take you home," Matthew pleaded.

"No, thank you," Jessica said. "I'll be fine, Matthew. And there's no reason you shouldn't open The Secret Garden today."

She didn't want to tell Matthew that she wasn't going home. And she certainly didn't want to risk him getting involved any more than he already was. She had heard Mark tell Matthew that he was going to need to talk to him again about the murder, as well, and it just compounded her worry.

Matthew hesitated, but then agreed. "Okay," he said, "Go get some rest. I'll keep an eye on things over here and work with the sheriff to make sure everything gets cleaned and locked up for you. And I'll see you in the morning."

"Thank you for everything, Matthew," she said. She wanted to hug him, but it also suddenly felt like maybe it would be inappropriate or forward. So, she waved, gathered her purse, and walked across the street to her car. "See you in the morning," she called out to Matthew who stood on the front porch of his shop as she drove away.

On the road, she headed toward the Amish community. She remembered visiting Anna and Beth one time several months ago, and she hoped she could remember the directions to their home again. And she hoped that they would be home and up for a surprise visit, as well.

She found the matching houses easily, sitting side by side, and pulled into the dirt driveway. Shifting her car into park, she had no sooner turned off the engine and stepped out of the car when Anna appeared on the front porch, waving to her.

"Jessica! Good morning!" Her voice was cheery, but she wore a look of undeniable concern on her face.

"Hi, Anna! You're a sight for sore eyes, I'll tell ya!" Jessica said, walking briskly toward the house and mounting the steps quickly. She hugged Anna tight. "Where is your sister?" she asked.

She's home, cleaning up after breakfast. "Good heavens, though, please tell me why you're here and not at the diner," Anna said, her forehead wrinkled.

"Well, that's the reason I'm here, I'm afraid." She looked at Anna and said, "It's not good, Anna. It's not."

Anna bit her lip. "Please tell me, I'm so sorry to hear this, and I want to know how I can help."

"I thought I heard talking out here!" Beth called out as she approached from the side of the house. "Anna, you didn't tell me Jessica was coming over," she teased her sister.

"Hi, Beth," Jessica said. "I'm glad you're here. I need to talk to both of you."

"Why aren't you at the diner?" Beth asked, "Is everything okay?"

Jessica shook her head, "No, I'm afraid everything is really not okay. I need your help more than ever right now."

Anna gently grabbed each of them by their arms and ushered them into her living room. "Let's have a seat. Does anyone want some tea?"

Beth and Jessica both politely declined as they got settled on either end of the couch. Anna sat on the upholstered chair next to them.

Jessica took a deep breath and told the sisters everything, starting with all the details she remembered about the robbery and to the last conversation she had with the sheriff. The sisters sat quietly and took it all in, handing Jessica a clean handkerchief and gently touching her arm or knee as she needed comfort telling the worst parts of the story.

"I'm so scared, Anna and Beth," Jessica said, tears flowing freely down her face as she wrung the handkerchief in her hands. "I have so many unanswered questions running through my head, and now I'm scared that whoever did this is trying to frame me. Or that Matthew might somehow get blamed."

Beth reached over and patted her hand, "I'm so sorry, Jessica, that this is happening, but take it from me, imagining the worst that can happen is not good for anyone in times like this. Your mind will run through all of the worst-case scenarios if you let it, but we can help you sort this out." She looked at Anna.

Anna nodded. "*Jah*, we can try to help you get to the bottom of this, Jessica, but Beth is right. There is no sense in worrying about terrible things that haven't happened yet. We need to focus on the facts."

Jessica nodded and wiped the tears from her eyes, "I know you're right," she said. "I just don't know how to turn off my mind."

Beth stood up and grabbed a pad of paper that had been pushed between two books on Anna's bookshelf. "Well, let's start working it out. That's the only way I can ever settle my mind. I have to get it out of my mind and onto paper. It may not solve everything, but it helps."

Anna nodded, "Yes, trust me. Beth knows what she's talking about." The women chuckled.

"I will get some tea. You grab a pen, Beth," Anna said, and within minutes the women were gathered at the table, ready to start their brainstorming session.

"Before we get started," Jessica said, "I just want to thank you. Thank you for being such wonderful friends and allowing me to just stop by unannounced and take over your morning. I know I thanked you for your help at the diner the other day, but I just want you to know that I consider the two of you more than just friends. You have become like family to me, and I would do the same for you anytime you need anything."

Anna and Beth smiled warmly at Jessica. "You are so welcome, dear. You have become like family to us, as well, and we want to help you. We care about you, so it's never a problem to stop by unannounced," Anna said.

Beth continued, "*Jah*, our doors are always open. Please don't ever hesitate to come by if you need anything."

Jessica took a sip of her tea and fought back tears. "I am so lucky to have you in my life. You see, I don't have any family. My mom passed away a few years ago, and my father walked away from us years before that. I don't think I mentioned it, but my mother's engagement ring was in the safe. The robber took that, too. It broke my heart because it was one of the only things I had left..." her voice trailed off as she worked hard to keep her composure.

Anna and Beth looked at each other and then back at Jessica.

"We didn't know any of this, Jessica," Anna said.

"And there's something we haven't told you," Beth spoke slowly looking at Anna to make sure they were on the same page. Anna nodded.

Jessica was curious. "What possibly could you have not told me?" she asked, confused.

"Well, when we were working at your diner the other day," Beth started.

Jessica leaned forward in anticipation.

Beth continued, "A man came in that said he was your ex-husband."

"*Jah*, a nice enough guy. James McLean, he said his name was," Anna agreed.

Jessica sighed. "Ugh," she said. "It's true. James is my ex-husband, but we did not leave things on good terms. He came in the other day, too, and I told him to leave me alone."

"He was definitely there to see you," Beth said.

"I don't know why, though." Jessica was frustrated. "He thinks he is a master manipulator. He tries to play games with people's minds, but he doesn't have as much power as he thinks he does. He was raised in an affluent family in a town called Billingsley. That's where I grew up," she explained.

Beth nodded. "That's what he said," she exclaimed. "And now, my daughter's husband just got a job offer in Billingsley. I was going to ask what you knew about that place."

Jessica leaned back in her chair, "Oh, I know everything about that place," she laughed. "It's not a bad place. There are a lot of good people who live there, and there's another Amish community nearby, too." She remembered. "Do you know who your son-in-law is going to be working for?"

Beth nodded, "It's a family-owned leather smith shop. I don't know the family's name, but they've been in business for many years, I understand."

Jessica immediately knew who Beth was talking about. "Oh! The Walkers. They are a wonderful family. You can trust them with your daughter's family. I am surprised they are hiring, but it should be quite the compliment to your son-in-law to be chosen. They have a very successful business that extends throughout the county and maybe further now."

Anna reached for the pad of paper. "Ok, somehow, Beth got us off track here," she teased her sister. "I don't mean to bring the mood down, but can we please refocus?"

Jessica and Beth smiled and agreed. They began taking notes of everything Jessica could remember. Then Jessica listed all the questions in her head. As she recounted everything for yet another time, she suddenly felt less overwhelmed and just very tired.

"Do you think we could just leave everything there for now?" Jessica asked. "I do feel so much better since we jotted everything down, but I think I could use some rest now."

Anna and Beth agreed. "Of course," Anna said.

"Rest will do wonders for you," Beth agreed.

Jessica gathered her purse and the sisters walked her out to the porch. They hugged her goodbye and watched her walk to her car. As she opened her car door, Jessica suddenly saw looks of concern cross their faces. The sisters began walking toward her, calling out something she couldn't understand, and she wasn't sure what was happening.

She thought things had begun to move in slow motion when suddenly, a young man in his early twenties appeared by her side. With one hand holding her car door propped open, he leaned in close to Jessica as she sunk into the drivers' seat. Through gritted teeth, Jessica heard him say, "You don't belong here."

"What?" she asked, in shock.

"You heard me. You'd better leave us alone," the young man said again. Jessica felt the hair raise on the back of her neck.

Anna and Beth swooped in, and the young man released the car door and stepped back. Anna scolded the young man, "Gabriel. What are you doing?"

Beth chimed in, "You should be ashamed of yourself! Now, get out of here before we call your father."

Gabriel ran off down the walking path towards his home.

Anna and Beth turned their attention to Jessica. "Are you okay?" Beth asked.

"Please don't pay him any mind," Anna said. "That is not normal behavior in our community, and you certainly don't need that on top of everything else you have going on."

Jessica nodded. "I'm okay," she said meekly. "I'll see you at the diner tomorrow?" she asked, hoping to assure the twins that everything was fine.

"Definitely," Anna said.

Beth smiled but she couldn't hide the concern on her face, "Now, you go get some rest. We're going to see what we can find out so that we can put this horrible day behind us."

Jessica thanked the women and drove home. She managed to drink a full glass of water before kicking off her shoes and crawling into bed. She fell fast asleep as soon as her head hit the pillow.

Chapter Twelve

T he heavy back door of the Little Valley Pub slammed shut behind Archer Melgren as he walked into the dark storage room. He resented working at the bar, but he knew it was only a means to an end. And the end was getting closer and closer every day that he worked hard and stayed focused on his goals.

"That you, Archer?" Sam Graber's voice drifted from the front of the bar.

"The one and only," Archer replied as he walked in from the back. "How's it going, Sam?" He asked, cordially.

"Ah, you know. Living the dream," Sam said sarcastically. His hand wrapped around a glass of whiskey, and he was watching an afternoon Court TV show streaming through the large television above the bar.

Archer reached up and grabbed his dark green apron off the hook hanging just inside the short hallway between the shelved wall behind the bar and the storage room. "It's five o'clock somewhere, right?" He chuckled, teasing Sam about drinking at two o'clock in the afternoon.

Sam flashed him an annoyed look. He retorted, "You're a real funny guy, ain't ya?" Then doing a double take, he hollered out, "Whoa! Who gave you that shiner?"

It was Archer's turn to roll his eyes. "It's not what you think," he said. "No one gave me a black eye. I'm well past the age of fighting in the streets," he said.

Sam looked at him, standing on the rungs of the bar stool and leaned in closer. "It looks like a shiner to me," he said, chuckling. "Don't wanna admit you got your butt kicked, huh?" He took another swig on his whiskey and returned to watching his show.

Archer was relieved that Sam didn't pursue the topic any harder. He was not about to admit to one of the biggest bullies in Little Valley that he spent most of his life in fear of his cousin.

Archer would have never come to stay with his uncle if he'd known his cousin, Darren, was getting out of jail. The two were fighting again within minutes of seeing each other. Archer was always so confused as to why his cousin hated him so much. He wondered if Darren enjoyed terrorizing him simply because he was smaller and weaker, and he tried many times to call a truce and make peace. But Darren wasn't having it.

But, they were older now, and Archer simply had too much to lose. So, he vowed to himself to make sure that this throwdown he had with him the night before would be the last.

Archer shook his head to clear his mind. He began his prep, slicing limes and stocking the bar with cherries. He emptied the dishwasher, stacking the glasses carefully on the shelves, and started to count inventory.

Sam's Court TV show had ended and was replaced by the local newswomen's voice. "Breaking news. An unidentified body was found dead this morning in Heaven's Diner, on Main Street in Little Valley," she began.

Sam yelled out, "Wow! That's crazy!" and Archer turned to look at the screen.

"Shhhh," Archer said as he tried to listen.

"The victim was in his mid to late thirties with a tattoo of a black bird on his wrist." Archer's heart started racing. "The unidentified man was pronounced dead this morning, as a result of a gunshot to the head," The woman continued. "The police do not have any current leads at this time."

Sam tapped his empty glass to signify to Archer that he needed another drink. "Well, I'll be damned," Sam said. "Another murder in this little ol' town. There's no doubt they'll be stopping by here to ask me where I was this morning," Sam said. "As a matter of fact, I can't believe they haven't already tracked me down." It almost sounded like Sam was proud of that. He wore being the meanest guy in town like a badge of honor.

How hard would it be to find you, Archer thought to himself, but he refrained from responding.

Plus, he had other things to worry about now. Archer knew that Sam had nothing to do with this. The victim was his cousin, and he wondered if his Uncle Jack had seen it on the news yet.

"Well, I think we're all ready to open now," Archer mumbled to Sam who wasn't really paying attention. He had found a daytime talk show to stare at while he nursed his next drink. "I'm gonna go take a quick break before we open," Archer said, not expecting a response.

He took off around the corner and stepped out the back door. He pulled his cellphone out of his pocket, his hands trembling slightly, and dialed his Uncle Jack's number. The phone rang and rang and went to voicemail. Archer hung up. He figured Jack was either still asleep from his afternoon nap, or he was simply ignoring the call. He waited a few seconds and tried again. This time, Jack answered.

"Yep," Jack said.

"Hey, Uncle Jack, it's Archer."

"I know. What's up?"

Uncle Jack never claimed to be much of a communicator. He was more of a "get straight to the point" kinda guy. Archer chanted *a means to an end* in his head before continuing. "I was just calling to see if you'd happen to have seen the news today."

"Nope," Uncle Jack said, annoyed. "I don't know if I have watched the news in something like twenty years."

"Right," Archer said. He looked at his watch. He needed to open the doors in less than two minutes. "Well, I'll get right to the point then."

"That would be great," Uncle Jack said, yawning.

"They found a dead body in the diner on Main Street this morning," Archer said.

Jack responded before Archer could continue, "So?"

"So, it was Darren, Uncle Jack. Darren was shot in the head and left for dead in the diner," Archie said. The clock was ticking, and he needed to go, but he needed Uncle Jack to know about this.

Jack was quiet, and Archer's anxiety increased.

Archer said, "Uncle Jack? Are you okay?'

Jack made a noise that Archer couldn't distinguish, so Archer continued, "Here's the thing, though. The police don't know it's him. You need to go tell the sheriff it's Darren. And you need to tell him about all his enemies and everything."

"Well, if the police don't know it's Darren, then how the hell do you know it's him, Archer? Wishful thinking? Or did *you* kill him?" Jack responded in an angry tone.

Archer took a deep breath. "No, Uncle Jack. They mentioned his tattoo on the news. You know, the bird tattoo on his wrist?"

Jack scoffed. "Well, with his criminal history, they'll find out who it is soon enough. I don't gotta say nothing."

"You're probably not wrong," Archer said, "but you don't wanna get tied up in something you don't have to be. And maybe you know something that could help lead to the killer. You never know, I guess, but it's up to you. I just thought I should call you after I watched it on the news."

"Right. Did you say he was killed at the diner? Isn't that the place the McLean girl owns?" Uncle Jack asked.

"Yep," Archer said. "Jessica McLean owns the place."

"Interesting," Jack said pensively. Then, after a short pause he snapped, "Well, I'm sure you're happy as a lark right now, Archer," Uncle Jack said. And he hung up the phone.

Archer sighed loudly and shoved his phone back in his pocket. He was a few minutes behind schedule, and he didn't want Sam breathing down his neck about it.

Luckily, Sam was in the john when he slipped back into the storage room. He held the heavy door while it closed, so it didn't slam. Once secured, he snuck into the dining room to unlock the doors.

Settled behind the bar, waiting for customers, his mind wandered. Uncle Jack wasn't wrong. He was happy that Darren was out of his life forever. It's true his Uncle Jack was nice enough to let him stay with him for practically nothing, but Archer still deserved to be treated with respect.

Archer suddenly worried what this news might do to his uncle. If Uncle Jack fell off the wagon, Archer would need to find another place to stay. He hated how his life was always so erratic. He yearned for consistency, and he hoped that Darren's absence would make things just a bit better.

It's just a means to an end, he thought to himself, as he wiped down the bar.

Chapter Thirteen

T he sheriff looked up from his desk and a small smile
spread across his face. He watched with amusement
as a horse and buggy pulled up with two familiar faces
riding in the front.

"Looks like we have company," he told Deputy Jones,
pointing to the window as the women fussed over tying
the reins to the sawhorse planted at the bottom of the
porch steps.

Deputy Jones smirked. "I was wondering when they
were gonna get here," he laughed.

Sheriff Streen stood and opened the door just as Anna
and Beth reached the top step and set foot on the porch.

"Well, fancy meeting you here," the sheriff greeted them warmly.

"Hi, Sheriff," Anna and Beth said in unison. The sheriff had told the twins on more than one occasion that they could call him by his first name, Mark, but they chose to continue to call him Sheriff.

"Come on in! Can I pour you some coffee?" The sheriff leaned his back against the open door and stretched out his arm, inviting the twins inside.

"*Denki*, Sheriff, but I've had enough coffee already today," Anna responded with a smile as she passed him and walked inside.

Beth agreed and followed her sister.

"Good afternoon, Mrs. Troyer. Mrs. Miller," the deputy said courteously with a nod of his head.

"*Gut daag*," the women responded together before settling into the seats across from the sheriff's desk.

The sheriff rested in his large office chair and leaned back slightly. "So, to what do I owe the pleasure of your visit today, Anna and Beth?" he asked, with a grin although he had no real doubt as to why they were there. A murder had taken place, a body found, and their friend was involved. Those were the ingredients for the perfect case for the amateur sleuths.

"Well," Anna began, "we're here because we had a visit with Jessica yesterday."

The sheriff nodded. "Okay," he said, prompting Anna to continue.

Beth jumped into the conversation instead. "She told us about the man found dead in her diner, and how the police found a gun under her cash register."

"Yes, I know," Mark sighed. "If the two of you hadn't shown up today, we would've made a trip out to see you. We're still waiting for fingerprint test results and identification of the victim."

Beth nodded. "*Jah*, we didn't expect you to have those results back just yet," she said.

"Right," the sheriff said. He was thinking about how the two women had become quite knowledgeable about things like fingerprints and suspects over the last year. When he first met them, they had already been involved in solving the local murder of his predecessor. He was immediately impressed by the women's wisdom and stamina, especially when it came to fighting for justice for those whom they cared dearly.

"Well, you know Jessica didn't kill that man, don't you, Sheriff?" Anna asked pointedly, interrupting Mark's thoughts.

The sheriff and the deputy exchanged quick glances. The sheriff sincerely hoped that Jessica was innocent, but he was not ignorant to the ways of the world. He certainly could recall times from the past where he had been convinced that someone was innocent, and it turned out they were actually guilty. As a sheriff, he knew he had to keep his personal feelings for someone out of the picture when solving a case.

He was prepared to traverse the waters carefully with the twins. He knew they were willing to go to battle on Jessica's behalf, if they had to.

"I certainly don't want to believe that she did." He paused and rubbed his tired eyes. "We don't have enough to arrest her, but we also don't have many clues leading us to someone else right now."

The deputy interrupted. "Ms. McLean could've killed the victim in self-defense," he said. "I guess you know that we're pretty sure it was the robber that was shot and killed?" The deputy removed his hat and set it in his lap before tousling his hair.

Beth pivoted slightly in her seat to respond to the deputy. "Well, yes, Jessica told us about the tattoo on the man's wrist." She frowned and continued with a clear and steady voice. "I hear what you're saying about self-defense, Deputy, but Jessica says she did not shoot the victim. If it were in self-defense, why would she lie about it?"

"Right. That doesn't make sense," Anna agreed. "What clues *do* you have, Sheriff?"

"Well, like I said, there isn't much to go by just yet. We're waiting on fingerprints, and we've searched

Heaven's Diner high and low. There was no sign of forced entry. The back door was locked, and Jessica says the front door was unlocked when she arrived."

He continued, "Finding the gun stashed away under the cash register was not a good turn of events for Jessica, I'll admit. Especially when she had just told me she didn't own a gun. And, not knowing the victim's identity makes things exceptionally difficult to consider other suspects."

"I wish we had tested Jessica for gunpowder residue," the deputy said.

Mark nodded. "Yeah, me too. I was thinking that, as well. I'm worried that we'll regret not doing that," the sheriff said, rubbing his chin.

The phone on Mark's desk rang, and he grabbed the receiver.

"Sheriff's Office. This is Sheriff Streen," his words were rushed and full of anticipation.

On the other end of the phone was the officer from the scene of the crime earlier that day. "Hi, Sheriff. I just wanted to check in and see how things are going."

"Fine. Fine. We completed our search at the diner. We weren't able to find any additional clues. We had the cleaning crew come in, and we supervised that before locking up and heading out."

"Okay," the officer said. "Well, we're still waiting on test results. As you know, that's not typically a next day thing, but hold tight. We'll contact you just as soon as we have them."

"Yes, that sounds good," Mark said. "I realized I didn't give you my cell phone number earlier today. I have yours from the business card you handed me." He rattled off the numbers to the officer.

"Alright. I'll give you a call on your cell, then, as soon as anything new develops," the officer said. "You do the same, will ya?"

"Absolutely," Mark said. "Thanks for calling and we'll talk again soon." He set the receiver back down on the phone's base and looked over at the deputy, then towards Anna and Beth.

"No news yet," Mark said.

Deputy Jones stood to his feet and began pacing behind the sheriff's chair. "Well, now that you gave him your cell phone, we don't have to just sit here and wait for the phone to ring. I think we should go talk to Matthew Beiler again. Maybe with the right questions, he can remember something else."

The sheriff nodded, "Yes, I agree. Someone must have seen something and they just don't realize there's a connection. We'll start with Matthew."

Before he could encourage Anna and Beth to start asking around as well, an unfamiliar car pulled into the lot.

"I wonder who that is," Mark said, nodding toward the window.

The women turned in their chairs to look. Beth rose to her feet to get a better view as a man stepped out of the vehicle.

"Ah, that's Jack Melgren," Beth said. "He has lived here for a while. About ten years or so, would you say, Anna?"

Anna nodded, "Yeah, maybe about that. I can't remember exactly how long, but I know he's part of Sam Graber's circle of friends." She raised her eyebrows at Mark before finishing with, "If you know what I mean."

Mark had never met Jack, but he knew exactly what Anna meant. He was more than a little bit familiar with Sam Graber, the owner of The Little Valley Pub. Mark didn't know them all, but he knew there was a group of people, mostly men, that frequented the establishment, and he could only assume that Jack Melgren was one of them.

Jack opened the front door to the station and stepped inside. He was a tall man with broad shoulders, unkempt hair, and dark eyes.

"Howdy," he said, nodding at the sheriff. "I'm Jack Melgren." He reached across the desk to shake his hand.

"Mr. Melgren," the sheriff said, shaking his hand firmly. "I'm Sheriff Streen. This here's my deputy, Christopher Jones, and Anna Miller and Beth Troyer."

Jack nodded at each of them as they were being introduced.

Anna and Beth began donning their shawls. Mark assumed they either wanted to respect Jack's space and allow him privacy or they didn't like his kind and wanted to quickly retreat. Or maybe both.

"How can I help you, Mr. Melgren?" The sheriff asked as the women picked up their purses.

Jack got straight to the point. In an even tone, he stated, "Well, I'm here because my nephew saw on the news that my son was found shot to death in Heaven's Diner yesterday mornin'."

The twins froze and silence hovered over the room. All eyes were on Jack's face as he looked at the floor and stuffed his hands in his pockets.

Jack continued in the same unemotional voice. "His name was Darren. Darren Melgren. He was thirty-four years old."

Still, no one in the room moved. If a pin had dropped on the floor, it's impact would have been clear as a bell.

"Ok," Mark said, exhaling slowly. "Can I ask you, sir, why you think the man we found is your son?"

Jack looked up and locked eyes with the sheriff as he answered, "Because the news said the guy had a tattoo. Darren had a tattoo on the inside of his right wrist. It was a picture of a black bird. Its wings were spread wide open as if it were flyin'."

Jack continued, "And because he had been stayin' with me for a few days. He got outta jail and was layin' low at my house. He didn't come home last night."

Chapter Fourteen

Anna and Beth excused themselves and ducked out of the sheriff's station to allow for the sheriff and the deputy to continue questioning Jack Melgren. Before leaving, Anna had leaned over, and the sheriff heard her whisper to the deputy that the two of them would head to The Secret Garden to talk to Matthew and that they would connect again the next day to compare notes.

"Please have a seat," the sheriff offered to Jack. "Can I interest you in a cup of coffee?"

Jack settled into the chair that Anna had occupied minutes before and slipped his arms out of his jacket. He shook his head. "Nah, I'm good," he said.

Deputy Jones leaned forward. "I'm sorry for your loss, Mr. Melgren," he said respectfully.

Jack responded with a blank stare and remained quiet.

Mark was a bit confused by the lack of emotion, and he was ready to dive deeper. "Well, I guess since you dropped by, I'll assume you don't mind if I ask you some questions," the sheriff began, handing a pad of paper and pen over to the deputy.

Jack nodded, looking down at his hands in his lap, pulling at the cuticle of his fingernail on his right thumb. He looked up at the sheriff and said, "Sure, go ahead. What d'ya wanna know?"

Mark leaned forward. "Well, let's start with this," he said. "Do you know who would want Darren dead?"

Jack scoffed. "Where do I start?" He cracked a smirk, exposing a mouthful of crooked yellow teeth. "Jack was never the most popular kid."

The sheriff nodded, waiting for more.

Jack continued, "I don't know why you're asking me that, though. I thought it was pretty obvious that the McLean girl is the one that killed him."

The sheriff was surprised to hear this statement from Jack, but he remained emotionless and still.

"You know, her ex and Darren were childhood friends back in Billingsley, right?" Jack said.

The sheriff did not know that, but he nodded as if it were not news.

"That's right," Jack continued. "I never liked Jimmy McLean, and I warned Darren that he was going to get in trouble hanging out with that kid. Jessica really hated Jimmy hanging out with Darren when she and Jimmy were married, too." He wiped his palms on the sides of his pants.

The sheriff noticed and realized for the first time that Jack was nervous. Wanting to put him at ease, the sheriff asked, "So, tell me about Darren. What was he like? Were the two of you close?" The sheriff hoped that showing some kind of interest in Jack's son would build trust with the victim's father.

Jack grew quiet for a minute and wiped the palm of his hand on the back of his neck. "I don't know. Darren's mama died when he was a kid, so it was just me and him mostly. I wasn't the best dad, I'll admit. I kinda had a, um... well, I drank a lot back then." He stopped and looked from the sheriff to the deputy and then back to the sheriff again and said, "I mean, I'm sober now. Six months and eight days since I had my last drink."

"Congratulations," Deputy Jones said. "That's commendable. My dad went through that same thing. I know it's hard."

Jack shot him a look of appreciation before continuing, "Well, I wish I had quit a lot sooner. Darren started acting out real young, back when we lived in Billingsley. He was a good kid, I know he was. He just was so weak when it came to peer pressure, is all.

"He started messing 'round with drugs, and he became a drunk. Like his dear ol' dad," he cringed. "He spent the last twelve years in and out of jail and prison, but I don't believe he was ever the mastermind behind any of those crimes."

The sheriff was taking notes: *Jimmy McLean, Billingsley, Jail/Prison.*

Jack shook his head. "You know, he just got that tattoo before he got out, he told me, because that was his dream. He wanted to be free and fly away from all of it, like that bird." He paused. "It's ironic, ain't it?"

"How do you mean?" the sheriff asked.

"Well, it was that bird that identified him," Jack explained.

The sheriff nodded and prompted Jack to continue talking by asking him, "So, when did he come home last, and what was he like? Was he sober?"

Jack snorted, "Ah, hell no. He wasn't sober." He laughed and slapped his leg. "Now, that's funny," he said. Then, as if he realized he was the only one laughing, he pulled himself together and grew serious again.

"He came home just a few days ago, acting all shady like he was trying to hide or somethin'... I even asked him if he got let out for real or if he escaped. I wasn't about to house no fugitive." Jack watched as the sheriff scribbled on the pad again.

He leaned forward and waved his hand as if he wanted the sheriff to dismiss that thought. "He wasn't though. Hidin', I mean. He had done his time and they let him go."

The sheriff nodded. He wanted to ask how he knew for sure, but he realized it didn't matter. He'd investigate that on his own later.

"Yeah, you know my nephew Archer who works at Graber's pub, right?" Jack asked.

The sheriff cocked his head slightly. He hadn't yet made the connection that Archer was Jack's nephew. "Yeah, I know Archer. He seems like a good kid."

Jack did not confirm nor deny that statement and instead he said, "Well, Archer has been staying with me for a few months now. I don't think Darren knew that when he got here. I know I never told Darren about it."

The sheriff was intrigued to find out what role Archer played in this.

"You see, Archer and Darren never were really friends. Archer is a couple years younger than Darren, and he was always kinda scrawny and nerdy compared to Darren. The

kids picked on him in school, and well, so did Darren."
Jack began picking at his cuticle again.

"I guess maybe I give him a hard time, too, but man, that kid needed to learn to stand up for hisself, really. He's not gonna get very far in life, always being such a pushover. That's why he's got all those money problems now. He let somebody take advantage of him."

The sheriff refrained from taking notes, not wanting to distract Jack, and held eye contact, hungry to hear more about this family dynamic.

"Besides all that, though," Jack continued, "I think Darren always felt like Archer thought he was better than Darren. And I'm not so sure he was wrong, to be honest.

"The other night when Darren came home," Jack readjusted his position in his chair, stretching his legs out in front of him under the sheriff's desk and crossing his ankles, "he saw Archer sitting on the couch. It was Archer's weekend - that's what we call it when he's got a couple days off in a row - and we was watching the Vols play the Gators."

Jack shook his head, remembering that night. "Darren set eyes on his cousin and just lost it. He wanted to know what Archer was doing there, and Archer asked him the same thing. I wish you coulda seen the scared look on Archer's face. I'll tell ya, hee didn't know Darren was comin' over. And I didn't know it either, though."

The sheriff and the deputy listened closely without interrupting. Jack didn't need anyone to encourage him to continue at this point. It was as if he was on a roll.

"So, Darren came in, called him some names and grabbed lil' ol' Archer by the collar and stood him right up on his feet." He chuckled. "I don't mean to laugh, but Archer looked like a damn rag doll, I'll tell ya."

Looking down at his hands, Jack stifled his laugh and composed himself. "So, before I could get in the middle of those two boys, Darren had thrown a punch and damn near broke Archer's nose. Archer fell back on the couch all dramatic like and I pushed Darren down the hall to my room."

Jack paused as if he couldn't remember what he was going to say next.

"That was good of you, Mr. Melgren. To intervene, I mean," Deputy Jones said.

Jack nodded and then said, "Yeah, thanks. I've been pretty much saving Archer from Darren his whole life."

The sheriff said, "So, then what happened after that? What did Darren do?"

Jack shrugged, "I told him if he was gonna stay there, he had to promise to leave Archer alone. And he did, I think. Well, he basically just kinda stayed away from him, for the most part. He wasn't there a whole lot. He stayed home, mostly sleeping during the day and then hung out with me at night. "'Cept that first night, I know he took the car out real late, because the keys were on the kitchen table when I got up. I never leave the keys on the kitchen table. I got a bowl on the counter where I always put my keys."

"Do you know what night that was?" the sheriff asked.

Jack shrugged. "I think it was Monday night. Wait, what's today?"

"Today is Friday," the sheriff said. The sheriff thought that there was a good chance they were talking about the night of the robbery. He exchanged a knowing glance with the deputy.

"Do you remember anything particular about last night?" Deputy Jones asked.

Jack shook his head. "Nah. Honestly, I didn't even know he had gone out until I got up in the middle of the night to get a glass of water. I happened to notice that the back door wasn't locked, and I know I locked it before I went to bed. I always lock up before I go to bed, and Archer doesn't get home till real late. He closes up at the pub. I looked out the window to see if my car was gone, but it wasn't. It was parked in the driveway. My keys were in the bowl. So, Darren must've gotten a ride, I figured. I went ahead and left the door unlocked in case he couldn't get back in. And I left a note for Archer to leave it unlocked, too."

Jack fidgeted in his seat, and the sheriff thought he looked tired.

"One last question, Mr. Melgren, if you will." The sheriff asked permission and Jack nodded.

"How did you say you found out about Darren's murder?"

"Archer told me it was on the news. He said that the news girl mentioned Darren's tattoo," Jack said. "He said I should come in here and that I could possibly help you find the killer."

The sheriff set down his pen.

"But, like I said, I just assumed it was Jimmy's ex-wife. I mean, it was *her* diner where he was shot. And they've got that history. I figured she probably found out Darren was here and didn't want him in Little Valley. All those bad memories and all," Jack said, standing to his feet and pushing his arms into his jacket, one by one, before pulling the zipper up to his neck.

"Well," the sheriff said, "We're still collecting evidence. I'll let you know what we find out, though, Mr. Melgren, and we'll let the authorities know you've come in. They'll be in touch with you, too, for identifying Darren's body when you can."

Jack hung his head, "Right, okay. Thanks, Sheriff. Let me know if I can do anything else."

"You've done a really good thing by coming in here today, Mr. Melgren," Deputy Jones said. "Take care of yourself," he said as he escorted him out the door.

Shutting the door, he turned to the sheriff. "Wow. That was a lot."

The sheriff nodded, sitting back down, and pulling his cell phone out of his pocket. He punched the numbers on the business card in front of him into the keypad. The officer answered right away.

"Hi, it's Sheriff Streen from Mainstay County."

"Hi, Sheriff. What's up?"

"We know who the victim is. His father just left our office," Mark told the officer.

"Weird. I was just about to call you and tell you we got a positive ID on ex-con Darren Melgren."

Chapter Fifteen

Beth parked her horse and buggy outside The Secret Garden. Glancing across the street at Heaven's Diner, she was hit with a wave of emotion as she noticed the sign reading closed still hung on the door.

"Anna, look," she said, pointing to the building.

Anna turned to see and said, "Oh, that's *baremlich*. I just assumed Jessica would reopen it today. I hope she's okay."

"There's her car, so she must be in there," Beth said. "Maybe she's just going to open late."

Anna nodded, "*Jah*, maybe that's it. I hope the cleaners did a *gut* job on the place yesterday. Let's go check on her after we visit Matthew."

Beth agreed and the two of them hitched up the horse to the stake in front of the flower shop and headed inside.

Opening the door, Anna called out, "*Gute mariye*, Matthew!"

Matthew and Moses Schrock came around the corner from the back room, smiles on their faces. "*Gute mariye*, Anna and Beth! *Wie bischt*?" Matthew greeted the two sisters.

Moses owned the hardware store next door and was Matthew's closest childhood friend. He was also Anna's son-in-law, married to her oldest daughter, Sarah. He greeted them both warmly, as well.

"What can I do for you this morning?" Matthew asked, leaning on his counter. "Need some flowers for your next party?"

"Not yet," Beth said. "Our next party is Thanksgiving, and we have much more planning to do."

"But soon," Anna said. "We'll be ordering soon."

"Oh, Sarah mentioned that we are having a community-wide Thanksgiving dinner this year. I am looking forward to it," Moses said, clasping his hands together in front of him. "I'm already hungry thinking about it," he laughed, and the others joined him.

"We actually came by to chat with you, Matthew, about what happened yesterday. Jessica came by the house and shared her account of everything," Beth said.

Anna interjected, "We just want to make sure you're okay. I know it must have been traumatizing to find the body in the diner. Jessica mentioned how you were so supportive and took care of her."

Matthew blushed. Moses nudged Matthew's arm as if he were teasing him, and Beth thought they looked like little boys again for a few seconds.

"*Jah*, it was *baremlich*," Matthew said. "I'm glad Jessica was able to come by, though, and talk it out with the two of you. It's times like that when you really need good friends in your life."

"And it doesn't hurt when your friends are also really good at solving crimes," Moses smiled and winked at the twins. "So, tell us. Do you two already know who the victim is and most importantly, who we should be wary of around here?"

Beth and Anna exchanged glances before Beth answered. "Well, we just found out before heading here that the victim is Darren Melgren, Jack Melgren's son."

Matthew and Moses were both surprised at the news.

"Jack's son is the one who robbed Jessica at gunpoint?" Matthew exclaimed.

"*Jah*, that's what we heard, but it hasn't been confirmed by the police yet, as far as we know. Did you ever meet Darren, Matthew?" Anna asked.

Matthew shook his head.

"Me either," Moses said. "I don't think I even knew Jack had a son. I know that Jack is Archer's uncle, and that Archer is living with him."

"Oh, right," Beth said, again looking at Anna. She dreaded it, but she had a feeling they might be visiting Sam Graber's bar to talk to Archer later that day.

"I like Archer," Matthew said. "He has always been very friendly and respectful."

Moses agreed.

"Have you seen Jessica this morning?" Beth asked, nodding her head to the diner across the street.

Matthew nodded, "*Jah*, I saw her briefly this morning when she got here." He paused before continuing, "She is pretty shook up, as to be expected. I walked into the diner with her and sort of inspected the place to make sure she was safe. She said she was going to open late this morning. She needed some time alone in there, I think."

Beth sighed, "I know it must be very hard for her. She loves the diner, and it's just horrible that this happened there."

"I'm worried for her," Matthew continued, "and I know she is worried, too." He stood up straight. "The sheriff makes it sound like the police have their eyes on her as a suspect."

"Indeed," Anna confirmed, "I think they do."

Beth asked, "Do you know anything about the gun, Matthew?"

Matthew shook his head, "Nothing. I can't imagine that Jessica owns a gun."

"There has to be an explanation for that then," Anna said. "The sheriff is waiting right now for the fingerprint test results. We are holding our breath that someone else's prints are found."

"Of course someone else's fingerprints are going to be found. Jessica insists she has never owned a gun, let alone shot one," Matthew said, sounding defensive.

Beth locked eyes with him and recited an Amish proverb. *An honest heart is all that is needed for a prayer to reach the Lord.*

Matthew nodded and relaxed his shoulders.

"*Jah*, we are all praying for Jessica to escape scrutiny and definitely false accusations," Anna said, and everyone nodded.

"Is there anything else that you remember that you didn't report to the sheriff yesterday, Matthew?" Beth asked.

Matthew sat quietly for a moment before responding. "I wish I had thought of something else that could help Jessica," he said, hanging his head.

Moses reached out and patted his friend on the back. "Everything will work itself out, my friend. *Gotte* takes *gut* care of his children."

Matthew shot Moses a look of gratitude.

"Jessica mentioned that you said you showed up and gave her a fright before the two of you walked in together," Beth began again, hoping to help uncover something new by jogging Matthew's memory.

Matthew nodded and grinned. "I didn't mean to scare her. We had a good laugh over it."

"So, were you there before Jessica arrived then?" Beth continued.

Matthew shook his head. "No, I was running late that day. I had been arriving early each day before to watch as she opened the diner and make sure the robber didn't come back."

He stuffed his hands in his pockets. "But, yesterday, I was running late, and I decided to go over and say hello. I offered to walk her inside." He pulled his hands back out of his pockets and wiped his palms on his pants. "I didn't tell anyone this, but I was going to ask Jessica on a date again."

The twins smiled and nodded in unison.

Matthew looked down at the counter in front of him as he spoke. "We had planned to go on a date earlier in the week, but she had canceled it because of the robbery. She said she was afraid she wouldn't make for good company." Matthew looked up and waited for the twins to respond.

There were a few seconds of quiet before anyone spoke again.

"Okay, well, did you ever see anything out of the ordinary on the days you arrived earlier? Think back even to the morning Jessica was robbed. Did you see anything strange or anyone that you don't know?" Beth decided to not address the dating topic and instead circle back to the investigation.

Matthew was quiet and began to shake his head but stopped as he remembered something.

"Actually, I do remember seeing some guy I don't know come into the diner. He passed me as I was leaving. I held the door open for him."

Anna and Beth leaned forward slightly.

Matthew continued. "He was dressed smart, like a businessman, and I happened to glance back as he walked in. He went straight up to Jessica. She was at the counter. And I could be misreading things, but she looked like she had almost seen a ghost when she laid eyes on him.

"I kept an eye on things from across the street here a little bit, as best as I could. He wasn't there long. I saw him come out and get into a fancy red car and drive off," Matthew said. "I never asked her anything about it. I actually forgot about the whole thing until just now."

Beth knew that Matthew was talking about the same man that Anna and Beth met while they were working at the diner, Jessica's ex-husband. Realizing that Jessica had not mentioned anything about her ex to Matthew already, she decided not to share her thoughts aloud. Looking over at Anna, she knew that the two of them were in agreement again.

"Ok, well, that's good then," Anna said. "We'll let you two get back to business. We're gonna go check on Jessica and see if there's anything more we can do to help."

Beth thought Matthew looked relieved for the conversation to end, and he wished the sisters a good day. "Let me know if you hear anything new, will you, please?" Matthew asked politely.

"*Jah*, of course. Just keep watching over our friend in the meantime, will ya?" Anna asked with a grin.

Beth chimed in, "*Jah*, Jessica needs a guardian angel like you in her life right now."

Matthew blushed again as he and Moses followed the sisters outside and watched Anna and Beth cross the street.

Chapter Sixteen

Anna and Beth peered inside past the closed sign and saw Jessica standing behind the counter, her head down, deep in thought as she wrapped silverware. They knocked softly on the glass and waved.

Jessica's face brightened with a smile as she walked briskly to the door to greet the twins.

"Come in!" she said excitedly, as she unlocked the door and opened it wide.

"*Gut* morning," the sisters said in unison.

"Hi! Hello! I'm so glad you're here," Jessica said, giving each a quick hug.

Beth wrinkled her nose at the stench smell of bleach that lingered in the air. "How are you feeling this morning?"

she asked Jessica.

"I'm a little better. I'm getting ready to open, but it still smells so bad in here. I am hoping that it dissipates a bit before the lunch rush hits." She paused and looked down at the floor, "That is, if I still have customers. I'm not sure anyone wants to come eat at a place where someone was murdered. And it's all over the news."

Beth squeezed Jessica's arm tenderly. "Have faith, my friend. This too shall pass," she said softly, her eyes kind and compassionate.

Anna nodded. "As for the smell, all you need to do is to drop a couple teaspoons of vanilla into a dish and stick it in the oven at three hundred degrees for an hour. Turn your air vents on high, and the place will smell wonderful. Here, I'll go set that up for you now," she said, rushing off to the kitchen.

"Oh, my gosh, thank you so much," Jessica said. "You two are such wonderful friends! I am so grateful to have you in my life."

Beth smiled and responded, "We feel the same way about you, Jessica. Do you have time to sit and talk for a few minutes? I know you're busy. Or we can help in the kitchen again if you need us."

Jessica shook her head and gently escorted Beth to the counter. "No," she said firmly. "The two of you have done enough. I only have a little bit of prep work left before I'm ready. I would just love the company if you have time to visit."

Beth settled in a tall seat on the dining room side of the counter, and Anna came out from the kitchen and joined her.

"The vanilla is in the oven and the fans are on. You're all set now. The place should smell like Heaven in about an hour," Anna smiled.

"Or like Heaven's Diner," Beth joked, and the three of them giggled.

"Ah, it feels good to smile and laugh again," Jessica said, "but it makes me nervous at the same time. I still can't believe someone was murdered here, and I tossed and turned all night worried that I am going to get blamed for it."

The twins nodded with understanding.

"We've been praying for you, and for the victim, too," Anna said. "We met with the sheriff and deputy this morning, and we're going to do whatever we can to help get to the bottom of what happened."

Beth squirmed in her chair, she couldn't wait to share everything with Jessica. Anna turned to her and nodded, as if to give her the floor.

"So, we found out who the victim is," Beth said, excited.

Jessica stopped what she was doing and looked at Beth, her eyes wide. "Really? Who?"

"It's someone named Darren Melgren. He's Jack Melgren's son," Beth said, leaning forward.

Jessica gasped, and the color in her face drained.

Beth and Anna exchanged looks of concern.

"Wait. Do you know Darren?" Anna asked Jessica pointedly.

Jessica nodded, her eyes were cast down at the counter. Beth noticed her hands had begun to tremble. The twins waited for Jessica to explain.

"He was James' friend. They grew up together," she said quietly.

"James, your ex-husband?" Beth asked for confirmation gently.

Jessica nodded. "He wasn't a nice guy. I had no idea it was him," she was piecing her thoughts together, "but, now that I think about it, I remember feeling a hint of familiarity that morning he robbed me. I couldn't put my finger on it."

She looked straight ahead, her face flushed. "I haven't seen him in years. I thought he was in prison."

Her thoughts continued to ramble, and the twins watched as her emotions changed quickly.

"Oh, my gosh, I can't believe he did that to me," she said angrily, her eyes had turned darker, and her forehead was wrinkled. "I mean, I don't even care about the money, but he took my mom's ring!"

Anna reached out, grabbed Jessica's hand, and squeezed it tenderly.

Jessica looked from Anna to Beth and back to Anna.

"I don't know why they're in Little Valley all of a sudden," she said, sounding defeated. "I thought it was weird that James showed up, but now Darren was here, too?"

She shivered. "I hate not knowing what they're up to, but you never know with those two." She let go of Anna's hand and pressed her palms into the counter leaning forward. "They're dangerous," she said in a loud whisper.

Then, pulling her arms back to hang by her side, she balled her hands into fists and said, "I left Billingsley a long time ago to start a new life and put all of that behind me." She paused. "And now I find out they followed me here."

Beth's heart was racing, and she looked over at her sister. Anna reached out and took Beth's hand into hers under the counter.

Anna spoke, "Take a deep breath, please, Jessica."

"*Jah*, we've never seen you like this," Beth said nervously.

Beth's words seemed to shake Jessica out of it, and she immediately apologized to the twins. "I'm so sorry," she blushed. With a calm and controlled voice, she continued.

"You caught me by surprise. I'm not usually like this. Not anymore. I have been through so much with James. I moved here to put it all behind me and move on. My life in Little Valley has been wonderful. There is no stress, no fear, and no worries. Once James showed up, I worried that I was losing all of that. And now I see that I kind of have."

She wiped away a tear.

"I mean, I didn't like Darren at all, but I didn't want to find him dead in my diner. And now, I am also being looked at as one of the suspects. I feel like I'm losing all control over my life again," she said meekly.

Beth didn't have the heart to correct her and tell her that she wasn't just one of the suspects, she was the main suspect. And it didn't help to find out that she not only knew the victim, but that she really didn't like him either.

Beth squeezed Anna's hand. They were going to have to help her, but in order to do that, they were going to have to find out more about her past.

It was as if Anna read Beth's thoughts. She spoke kindly, "We can help you, Jessica. I know we can. But you'll need to tell us more about your past."

Jessica nodded and took a deep breath, exhaling slowly with her eyes closed. She began to recount her life story to the twins, telling them again how her father left her and her mother when she was a teenager. How her mother struggled to raise her on her own and how Jessica fell in love with James.

"I was so young, and lost. He promised the world. James' family was very wealthy, and they gave James everything he wanted. They probably still do," she said, rolling her eyes.

"We had a magnificent wedding. It was very lavish and just beautiful. But I'll never forget overhearing James' mother tell him how disappointed she and his father were that he had picked me. James wanted so badly to impress his parents, especially his mother, that the talk upset him pretty badly. He proceeded to drink way too much at the reception and pretty much ruined the whole thing."

She took another deep breath. "That night, the first night we were husband and wife, I saw a different side of him."

Beth was overcome with sympathy for Jessica as she continued telling her story.

"You see, everyone loves James when they meet him. On the outside, he's charming, attractive, and appears to be kind and thoughtful. That is the James I fell in love with all those years ago." She grabbed a glass off the shelf behind her and filled it with water from the sink in front of her. Taking a gulp, she swallowed and continued.

"There's another side to James. I've seen it. And his parents have seen it. And Darren has seen it, too," she said, her eyes cast down to the counter again.

"He can be mean and say the most hurtful things. Words that just drive right to the core of a person. The crazy thing is that he just gets away with it. He has a way of sort of making things right a lot of the times, making it somehow easy to just forgive everything. I've seen it with his parents, and especially with Darren. And I fell for it, too, for many years." Jessica took another drink of water.

"I finally woke up one day and decided I deserved something better. I moved back in with my mom and filed for divorce. The divorce quickly became messy. Even though his family never really wanted James to marry me, they really didn't want me to divorce him. They worried that it would tarnish their family's reputation, so they really just tried to destroy me. I ended up walking away with only my dignity. I didn't get any of his money or anything like that. And in the end, I was fine with that. I just wanted to walk away." Jessica looked at the twins, her eyes were soft and sad.

"My mom got sick during all of that. She was diagnosed with cancer, and she was in a lot of pain. I took care of her. We didn't have much. I worked at a small nursery part-time to help pay the bills for those few months, hating every time I had to leave her to go to work. One day," Jessica swallowed back tears, "I came home from work, and she was gone. She had passed away in her sleep."

Beth wiped away a tear of her own. "I'm so sorry, Jessica," she said.

"Thank you," Jessica said to Beth, with a look of gratitude.

"I didn't know it at the time, but it turned out that she had taken out a life insurance policy for me when my father had first left. And there was enough money for a nice small funeral to commemorate her life, and for me to purchase this diner. I know, it may sound harsh, but her passing really turned out to be a blessing in disguise. Her pain was over, and she and I could move on to better things. In my heart, I know she is in heaven right now, and that's why I named this place Heaven's Diner." A large smile spread across her face.

Beth clasped her hands in front of her, "Oh, that is wonderful! A blessing indeed!" She exclaimed, excited to hear the happy ending.

"Well, we can see now why you were so upset about your ex-husband arriving here in Little Valley," Anna said, and after a quick pause, she continued, "but now, we've got to figure out why he has decided to step back into your life. And what Darren has to do with this."

Jessica nodded. "I know. There's no doubt that James is the mastermind behind something shady. Darren was always his scapegoat, his accomplice. James had all the ideas, and Darren did all the dirty work." She continued,

"But why would James and Darren rob me? It doesn't make sense."

"*Jah*, I think if we find the answer to that, we may have the final clue we're looking for," Beth said. Then, speaking directly to Jessica, she asked, "Is it okay if we share your story with the sheriff? I think it could possibly bring a lot of insight to the case."

Jessica nodded. "Yes, I fully trust Mark, and I trust you two, of course. Plus, I'm willing to do whatever I need to put this all behind me."

Beth and Anna said goodbye and agreed to keep Jessica posted with whatever new clues they may find. As they headed out the door, Beth turned to Anna and said, "The vanilla worked! It smells *wunderbaar* in here now."

Anna smiled. "*Jah*, it's a good reminder that there's a solution for every problem."

Chapter Seventeen

Sheriff Streen pulled his car into the parking lot next to the Little Valley Pub. He parked right next to a shiny red Chevrolet Corvette. Reaching in the backseat for his cowboy hat, he remarked, "Well, that's a fancy car."

"Yeah, it is," Deputy Jones agreed. "I wonder who around here is driving that thing."

"Well, something tells me we're about to find out," the sheriff said as he stepped out of the car.

The sheriff and the deputy headed into the pub. Pulling the door open, the sheriff blinked a few times to adjust his eyes to the dim lighting inside. Once focused, he could see Sam Graber sitting at the bar chatting with another fellow he didn't recognize. Archer was behind the bar.

"Hey, there, Sheriff," Archer called out. "Deputy."

Sam turned in his seat. "Well, what'd I say? I told Archer that you'd be in here asking me questions. Any time there's a crime of any kind, I'm always the first stop."

The sheriff approached and removed his hat, setting it on the bar. "Well, if I didn't know you better, I'd think you were bragging right now," the sheriff said, teasingly. In the corner of his eye, he noticed the stranger fidgeting in his seat.

"Yeah," Deputy Jones said, "How preposterous that we would have questions for you when something goes down, right, Sam?"

Sam rolled his eyes. "Look, I keep my hands clean these days."

Archer chuckled.

Sam glared at him, "What you laughing at, boy?"

Archer just shook his head and went back to slicing limes.

The sheriff walked around Sam and extended his hand out to the fellow sitting on his right. The man looked out of place wearing slacks, dress shoes, a crisply pressed button-down shirt and what appeared to be an expensive watch.

"Hey, there. You must be the owner of that fancy car out there," the sheriff said, reaching out with an invite to shake his hand.

The man looked up from his drink and nodded, gripping the sheriff's hand in his for a strong handshake. "Yeah, that's my ride," he said, grinning.

The sheriff thought he looked pretty comfortable. He second guessed his earlier thoughts that the man may have looked a little nervous.

"I'm Sheriff Mark Streen," he introduced himself. "This here's my deputy, Christopher Jones."

Deputy Jones and the man shook hands next, with friendly smiles.

"Nice to meet you. James McLean," he said, introducing himself next.

Ah. So, this is Jimmy McLean, the sheriff thought to himself.

"I'm visiting down from Billingsley and thought I would stop by and see my old friend, Archer, here, before heading back," James explained.

The sheriff glanced at Archer and caught him grimacing.

"Good to meet you," said the sheriff. "I guess you all won't mind if we join you for a bit?" No one answered the questions, but the sheriff and the deputy both settled on bar stools next to James anyway.

"Can I pour you two anything?" Archer asks, wiping the counter behind the bar.

"Sure, I'll just take a tall glass of water," the sheriff said. "I'm on duty and all," he winked at James.

"Same for me," the deputy said.

Archer turned to grab two clean glasses off the shelf and reached for the ice scoop.

The sheriff turned to James. "So, what brings you down here to ol' Little Valley, James?" The sheriff asked nonchalantly.

"Well, I got some business here," he said.

"Oh, yeah? What business are you in?" the sheriff asked, nodding thanks to Archer as he set the glass of water on the bar in front of him.

"My family is in real estate," James said proudly. "I'm just down here scoping out the market, seeing if there's anything worth an investment."

Deputy Jones interjected, "What a coincidence. My wife is a realtor. We moved here not too long ago, and she was just saying how the inventory is so low here. I'm afraid you might be wasting your time."

James took a drink slowly, staring straight ahead. "Well, yep, that's the conclusion I came to myself," he said, sounding irritated. "But I figured that since I came all the way down here, I'd check in on Archer. We grew up together, me and Archer."

"Well, that's a stretch," Archer mumbled.

"What'd you say, Archer?" Sam asked.

Archer shook his head and kept silent.

The sheriff turned to Archer. "So, your uncle came into the station this morning, Archer," he said, watching Archer's reaction closely.

Archer seemed unshaken. "Good, good. I told him he should go see you," he said.

The deputy spoke up, "I'm sorry for your loss."

Archer looked up and said, "Thanks, but Darren and I weren't exactly close." He shifted his eyes to look at James. "James and Darren were pretty much best friends, though. Isn't that right, James?"

James stared back at Archer, his jaw was set, and the sheriff thought he might have been clenching his teeth.

"Oh, is that so, James?" the sheriff said.

Sam chuckled.

"I wouldn't say we were best friends," James said. "We knew each other, and we went to school together, but the truth is we come from different worlds, Darren and me."

"Well, Archer here is his cousin," the deputy said. "You made it sound earlier like you and Archer were good friends."

James finished his drink and ignored the deputy.

"Want another one?" Archer asked.

James shook his head.

The sheriff could tell James was ready to leave, but he wasn't quite ready to let him walk away just yet.

"So, you used to be married to Jessica, huh?" The sheriff asked.

James turned to face the sheriff. "That's correct," he said confidently. "We were married for over ten years. Up in Billingsley."

"Ah," the sheriff said. "I really like Jessica. She's a good girl."

James cocked his head. "Yeah. It's a real shame what she's going through right now, with Darren being shot in her diner and all." He stared at the sheriff without flinching.

The sheriff took a drink of water. "It's true. A real shame. We're working hard to get to the bottom of it for sure."

"She never did like Darren," James said. "As a matter of fact, I think you could say that she really couldn't stand him. She used to hate it whenever Darren and I would hang out together."

The sheriff held James' gaze and responded in a cool tone, "I thought you just said that you and Darren didn't hang out."

The deputy rose to his feet and stood next to the sheriff. "That's right, Sheriff. I think you said that you come from different worlds. Did I hear that right?"

James exhaled and said sarcastically, "Alright, I guess you caught me. Darren and I were friends." He leaned forward. "Don't tell that to Jessica, though," he said with a wink.

The sheriff smiled and said, "Ah. I figured you might come around with the truth. Now, you want to share why you're really in town today?" He asked, raising his eyebrows.

James remained steady and said, "I already told you. I'm here on business." He stood to leave and said, "Any more questions, Sheriff?" A broad smile spread across his face.

"Just one more," the sheriff said. "Where were you early yesterday morning?"

"Hmm..." James acted like he was in deep thought. "I was at home in Billingsley," he said.

He looked over at Archer. "What do I owe you?" he asked.

"Seven fifty," Archer replied.

James reached into his front pocket to pull out his wallet when something shiny came out with it, falling to the hard floor with a small *ping* sound.

James, the deputy, and the sheriff all looked down to see a diamond ring laying on the floor between them. Looking up, the sheriff watched as all color drained from James' face.

The sheriff knew guilty when he saw it.

"Put your hands behind your back," the sheriff demanded. "You're under arrest for the murder of Darren Melgren."

Chapter Eighteen

The sheriff's car pulled up in the dirt driveway in front of Beth and Anna's homes. The twins were sitting on the swing on Anna's front porch, warm shawls wrapped around their shoulders. Beth was holding a pad of paper and a pen, scribbling notes as they chatted.

Mark and Christopher stepped out of the sheriff's car and called out, "Good morning!"

Anna and Beth grinned and welcomed them.

"Come in! I'll fix you two some coffee," Anna said and led the way into her home.

Beth and the men followed inside and settled in the living room among the couch and upholstered chairs.

"What are you two working on this morning?" Mark teased Beth as she dropped the pad of paper onto the coffee table.

She smiled, "We're planning our Thanksgiving dinner party. This year, the whole community is coming together for dinner. You and your families are welcome to join us if you'd like!"

"Well, that's quite the invitation. Thank you," said the sheriff, and Christopher agreed.

Anna brought cups of steaming hot coffee on a tray into the room and set it carefully on the coffee table. In the center was a bowl of candied pecans.

"I made your coffee just the way you like it," she smiled.

The sheriff took a sip and nodded, "Perfect. You know me well, Anna Miller." He smiled warmly.

Beth leaned forward, "Tell us everything. We're so anxious to hear what happened at the pub yesterday!"

Matthew dropped by the evening prior to let Anna and Beth know that the sheriff had arrested James McLean for Darren Melgren's murder. The twins were waiting with bated breath for the sheriff to come by and give them a play by play.

Mark settled into the couch and told them all about their encounter with James the day before at the Little Valley Pub.

"We hadn't even expected to see him there. We went to question Archer, as you know," he said. "I guess you could call it a blessing that he was there, too." He winked at Beth.

Beth nodded. "It's true. Blessings come in all shapes and sizes, you know."

"Did he confess to everything?" Anna asked.

"Well, not right away. It took a lot of coaxing," Mark admitted. "He called his fancy lawyer."

Christopher chimed in, "By the time we got back to the station, we had heard from the officers who were running the tests. Jessica's prints were not on the gun, but someone else's were."

Mark explained further, "We know now that the prints are James's, but we weren't sure then. Thankfully, his lawyer was smart enough to know that we were going to piece it together and have that circumstantial evidence in hand soon enough since we collected his prints right away after arresting him."

Christopher nodded.

"So, what was the motive? We think we've figured out that James set Darren up to rob Jessica, but we can't figure out why," Anna said, sitting on the edge of her seat.

Beth agreed, "*Jah*, at first, we thought he might be trying to get back with Jessica. Maybe be the hero or something, but then that didn't make sense because ultimately, we think that James probably killed Darren to frame Jessica."

"Well, you're not that far off," Mark said. "There's a missing piece that the two of you don't have yet."

Mark and Christopher exchanged glances before Mark continued, "And the irony of it is that the missing piece is right here in your community."

The sisters gasped and said, "What?" at the same time. They looked at each other, both confused.

"Yep. I'm not sure if you know that the McLean family is quite connected up there in Billingsley. And with connections comes image. There is an Amish community up there, just outside of Billingsley and I guess the McLean family feels like they're a bit better than the Amish," Mark paused. "Social status is what I'm talking about here."

The twins nodded, and Anna said, "We understand."

"Well, someone from your community here spread word up there that Matthew Beiler and Jessica are dating, and I guess there's some conflict about that on both ends. In the Amish community, as well as with the McLeans, only because Jessica used to be married to James, of course." The sheriff looked at both sisters cautiously, one at a time. "I don't mean any offense when I'm sharing this with you."

Beth waved her hand in the air. "Nonsense," she said. "The only thing surprising about this is that someone from this community started this whole mess. We're pretty sure we know who is behind it, but that's neither here nor there."

Anna nodded in agreement. "Please continue," she said.

Mark took a deep breath. "I guess the McLean family sent James down to deal with it."

"Aahhhh," Beth said, putting the pieces together. "You're right. We were pretty close. I guess James had Darren do his dirty work and then tried to frame Jessica for his murder, to keep Jessica and Matthew apart."

"That's it. James was also hoping that Matthew might also somehow be looked at as a suspect, too, as it turns out, but he wasn't able to tie that together in the end," Christopher elaborated.

"Well, I'm glad that Matthew was kept out of it, but I'm sad for Jessica. I hope that her business can recover, and she can finally move on with her life for good" Anna said.

"Yes, we feel the same way. We're planning on heading over there when we finish up here. We have a surprise for her," Mark said.

Beth raised her eyebrows.

"It's her mother's ring. We can give it back to her now that we have a confession." Mark smiled.

Anna and Beth squealed with delight.

"Oh, that's so *wunderbaar!*" Beth said, her face beaming.

"*Jah*, she will be so happy!" Anna agreed.

"Well, we appreciate you two stopping by and catching us up. We'll let you go so you can bring Jessica her gift," Beth said.

"Please tell her we said hello," said Anna, "and that we'll be there later to see her."

Beth nodded. "We have some pies and goodies to deliver, and we want to see how she's doing," she said.

The sheriff and deputy thanked them for the coffee and headed out the door. Beth picked up her pad of paper and she sat back down to pick up where they left off with the party planning.

Anna was pacing.

"What is the matter, *Schwester*?" Beth asked, a tad frustrated and just wanting to finish what they started.

"We have to talk to the bishop about this. He needs to know what happened," Anna said, wringing her hands. "I was just shocked to hear about that."

Beth agreed. "Well, I can see that you're not going to be able to focus on turkey, stuffing and mashed potatoes until we are able to put this thing to bed. So, let's go see if Bishop Packer is home."

Chapter Nineteen

M atthew knocked on the turquoise blue door. He straightened his hat and smoothed down his shirt, taking deep quiet breaths to calm his nerves.

The door opened and Jessica greeted him with a beautiful smile. Her wavy red hair was pinned back on the sides. She was wearing an emerald green sweater and a long black skirt. A folded camel-colored wool peacoat was draped across her bent arm in front of her, a cream-colored scarf in her hand.

"Hi, Matthew!" she said, excitement in her voice.

"Hi! You look beautiful," he said and immediately blushed. It wasn't encouraged to comment on a woman's looks in the community, and once again, Matthew was confused as to how to approach things with Jessica since she was an *Englischer* and he was not yet baptized.

"Thank you," she said kindly, setting his mind at ease.

"Shall I help you with your coat?" Matthew asked and Jessica graciously accepted the offer. She handed him her coat and slipped the scarf around her neck, turning her back to Matthew to slip her arms into the sleeves.

She doesn't seem nervous at all, Matthew thought to himself, hoping that his nerves would calm soon, as well.

"I'm excited to ride in the buggy," Jessica admitted. "I've never ridden in one and have always wanted to."

Matthew grinned. He extended a bent arm for Jessica to hold onto as they walked down the short front pathway to the road. Arriving at the buggy, he pointed to the step and held her hand as she stepped inside.

He walked around and jumped in effortlessly, directing the horse to move forward at an ambling gait.

"It's a beautiful night tonight," Jessica said. "Thank you so much for inviting me again. I am so sorry I had to cancel our date before."

"It's my pleasure," Matthew said, focusing on the road in front of them.

"So, where are we going?" Jessica asked curiously.

"I thought we would drive into Bentley and go to dinner there. I hear that Antoine's is a nice place to eat," Matthew said.

"That sounds wonderful," Jessica said. "I've seen that place, but I've never been there. Maybe we can take a walk on their main street after dinner. It's a cute little town."

"Certainly, we can do that," Matthew grinned.

The conversation fell quiet, and Matthew focused on the sounds of the clip-clip of the horse's hooves on the dry ground. "What do you think of your first horse and buggy ride?" Matthew asked.

"It's very comfortable. Very relaxing," Jessica said, smiling. "I could get used to this as a mode of transportation."

Butterflies gathered in Matthew's stomach. He tightened his grip on the reins.

Jessica turned to face him, "I wanted to say, Matthew, that I just really appreciate everything you've done for me the past few weeks. You were so supportive and brave through all that craziness, and it just meant a lot to have you there with me."

Matthew glanced over at her and smiled and nodded. "Of course," he said.

She continued. "It's honestly just embarrassing that all of that happened. I didn't want everyone to find out about my past quite like that," she said.

"I understand that," Matthew said. "It was really challenging coming back to the community and facing my past, as well."

"Yes, but you and I have never actually talked about it. You know that I am divorced, right?" Jessica asked, sounding relieved to finally say the words.

Matthew nodded. "Yes, I have heard that." He paused before continuing, "I don't judge you for your past. And it doesn't change the fact that I want to spend time with you."

Jessica sighed, "I'm glad to hear that, but I know that not all of your community is as understanding as that. And I don't want you to have to be put in a position where you're in the middle."

Matthew was quiet, so Jessica continued, "I guess what I'm trying to say is that I've grown very fond of you, but I understand if you can only be friends, Then I still want to be friends."

Matthew glanced over at Jessica and gave her another warm smile before looking back at the road. "I've grown very fond of you, as well," he said. "I want to see if our connection is special and if it extends past friendship. I trust in *Gotte* that he is leading me down the path I should be taking. I enjoy spending time with you, and I don't believe that is harming anyone."

Jessica grew quiet, and the two sat in silence as they approached the town of Bentley.

"We are almost there now," Matthew said.

"If we find out that we enjoy each other's company and we build feelings for each other, will we be able to make a commitment? I think I need to know that answer in order to protect my heart," Jessica persisted.

Matthew parked the horse and buggy in front of the restaurant and turned to Jessica, finally ready to answer her question.

"Jessica, I already have feelings for you. I look forward to seeing you every single day. I admire you as a woman, beautiful both inside and out. You make me laugh, and you are a wonderful listener. You care about others, and you touch people's lives." Matthew poured everything out, as it was finally falling into place in his mind. "I have thought long and hard about a future with you, and I believe that you will share my desire to put *Gotte* first."

Jessica nodded, her eyes lost in his.

"I honestly don't know what that looks like within my community. We can make this work, no matter what. I have decided to postpone my baptism until the pieces fit together in our relationship, but I am still true to my faith while I wait and see." Matthew explained. "If we decide to reside outside of the community, I will still remain very close with my friends and family there and practice the same views as I do now."

Jessica reached out and touched Matthew's hand. "You are a wonderful man, Matthew. I am so blessed to have you in my life. I would not be opposed to joining your community. In fact, it would be an honor. I am just not sure if my past will be a barrier."

Matthew's heart swelled hearing those words come out of the mouth of the woman he had fallen in love with, and he was overcome with relief to finally have the clarity he had been searching for. He turned his hand over to hold Jessica's hand in his own.

"There is an Amish proverb that says, *Faith produces a way of life that pleases Gotte*. We certainly can't go wrong if we just both have faith." Matthew said.

Jessica's face brightened. "Well, that's easy," she said, with a wink.

Chapter Twenty

T he weather was a perfect fifty-five degrees and sunny as all the men, women and children in the Amish community residing in Little Valley joined together to celebrate Thanksgiving Day.

The community had decided to use the Schwartz family's barn since it was the newest, built after a fire was set only months earlier. Not only was it the nicest and largest barn in the community, the barn-raising party they had organized was a memorable celebratory time, filled with happiness and joy. It made perfect sense to celebrate a day of gratitude there, as well.

Picnic tables butted up against each other in three rows along the length of the barn, adorned with flower arrangements, some with blue thistle and others with orange marigolds. The kids were gathered on the end of one table with crafting supplies, creating paper hats with turkey feathers.

The smell of wonderful food was almost enough to make anyone's stomach growl with hunger. Everything smelled so delicious. A few select men were chosen to carve the turkeys as the women finished setting the tables with enough plates, silverware, glasses, and napkins for everyone.

Beth and Anna worked side by side removing plastic wrap and slipping serving spoons and gravy ladles into the different dishes of food that each family prepared and brought to the dinner.

"It looks amazing," Anna said to her sister. "I don't know why we don't do this every year!"

"I know!" Beth said, beaming. "It's so much fun to have everyone together!"

Anna stopped and said, "I wonder if Mark and Christopher and their families will join us."

Beth grinned, "I hope so! And Jessica, too! I know she said she was coming, and Matthew was pretty excited about it."

Matthew stepped up behind them, "Hey, I heard my name. I hope you two are saying nice things about me," he teased.

Anna and Beth laughed. "Well, of course, we are," Anna said. "There's nothing bad to say!"

"The flower arrangements are just beautiful, Matthew," Beth said.

"I'm glad you like them. I can't cook, but I can contribute as many flower arrangements as you want to every party you throw," Matthew said, smiling.

Then, leaning in and lowering his voice, he gently pulled the two sisters together to form a small private circle. "Another thing. I want to thank you two for speaking to the bishop and the deacon on my behalf. Gabriel came and sincerely apologized to me today, and it's all water under the bridge now," he said, his eyes shining.

"Oh, that's *wunderbaar* news, Matthew," Beth said.

Anna nodded. "*Jah*, we're so glad to hear that," she said, squeezing his arm. "So, do you have any news to share with us about Jessica?" She winked.

Matthew threw his head back and laughed before leaning back in towards the sisters. "I guess it's no secret that I have decided to officially court Ms. McLean." A boyish grin spread across his face. "And we're talking to the bishop together about what that looks like with the community. It's all very complicated, but my faith remains the same in my heart, and she holds a strong faith as well. The best part is that she is open to making whatever decisions are necessary for us to follow protocol and find happiness together."

"Well, that's a perfect answer, if I've ever heard one," Beth said. "We'll keep you both in our prayers."

Anna joked, "Just so you know, Beth has been praying for Jessica to be able to join the community since the day we met her, I think." The three of them laughed.

"Well, she already feels like family," Beth said, grinning.

"*Jah*, there is no doubt about that," Anna said.

Both twins wished Matthew good luck as he was pulled away to help other men bring in more chairs.

A few moments later, Anna said to Beth, "Well, look who just walked in!"

Beth looked up to see Christopher Jones, his wife, and their two little blonde sons walk into the barn. She waved as she and Anna made a beeline to welcome them.

"Hello! I'm so glad you made it!" Anna greeted them.

"Hi there," Christopher said. "You remember my wife Suzanne, and my boys Billy and Stephen?"

"Ah, yes," Beth said. "It's great to see all of you again. Please make yourself at home!"

"Thank you so much for having us. Christopher says such nice things about you two all the time, and you have quite the reputation for your baking. It's our pleasure, really." Suzanne said. "Oh! And I brought a vegetable casserole. It's a favorite in my family, and the boys love it. It's called 'Swiss Vegetable Medley.'"

"Yum! That looks delicious," Anna said, guiding Suzanne to a place to set it down. She began to introduce her to the other women.

Beth turned to join them and almost ran right into Jessica. "Oh! Jessica!" she exclaimed, delighted to see her.

"I'm sorry I startled you," Jessica laughed. "Happy Thanksgiving, Beth," she said as she hugged her tight.

"Happy Thanksgiving, Jessica. It's wonderful to see you. How are you doing?" Beth asked.

Anna snuck into the conversation and stole a hug before she could answer.

"I'm doing really well. Thank you for asking. Life's back to normal now. It's so nice. My customers are back, business is booming, and life is good." She smiled a big smile before continuing, "And I'm so grateful for the two of you, especially today. Thank you for everything you have done for me. I can't say it enough."

Anna and Beth waved their hands in the air.

"Ah, no thanks are necessary, Jessica," Anna said.

Beth chimed in, "Seeing you happy is thanks enough."

A few moments later, Matthew swooped in and greeted Jessica, taking her off to show her the flower arrangements. Mark Streen and his wife arrived, and everyone was seated after a quick prayer of thanks.

Beth sat pensive, enjoying her full plate of food, feeling almost overwhelmed with happiness.

She turned to her sister. "We have so much to be grateful for this year, Anna."

Anna nodded. "*Jah*, it's true. With hardship comes healing, and with healing comes gratitude."

Beth agreed, "I couldn't have said it better. Even the worst times can simply be blessings in disguise."

Sneak Peek into Christmas Chaos in Little Valley

Beth dropped the pile of Christmas books she wanted to borrow onto the desk. Greg Wilson was quiet as he scanned each book, one by one. Beth could tell something was wrong.

"Is everything ok, Greg?" Beth asked, tucking stray strands of hair into her *kapp*.

Greg lifted his face to hers and said, "I'm sorry, Anna, I'm just really distracted today."

Beth smiled. "I'm Beth," she said. This certainly wasn't the first time that she had been mistaken for Anna, and vice versa. "Is there anything I can do to help?" She asked, concerned. Greg had always seemed so friendly when she had visited the library. She worried that something was really wrong.

"Well, please don't spread this around because I haven't told anyone yet," he paused.

Beth's curiosity was piqued.

"It looks like we're going to have to shut the doors at the end of the year," he said. His shoulders slumped forward, and he looked at the floor.

"That's horrible!" Beth said. "What are we supposed to do without a library in town?"

"Well, we don't have enough funding to keep the bills paid every month. No one seems to be interested in borrowing books anymore. Everyone is shopping at that new bookstore near Tulip Square, and the young kids around here are all reading on their phones and computers now." Greg explained.

Beth was broken-hearted. The library was one of her favorite places to visit ever since she was a kid.

Greg continued, "And as if that wasn't enough, we've been getting all kinds of weird letters in the mail with threats that someone is gonna come and shut it down themselves. One of the notes even mentioned setting the place on fire."

Beth gasped. "Did you tell the sheriff about it?"

Greg nodded. "Yes, but he can't do anything without knowing who's behind it all. He said he's going to try and follow up on it, but he doesn't have any leads, as far as I know."

"Well, let me talk to the sheriff. My sister and I have a knack for getting to the bottom of things like this. Maybe we can help," Beth said.

Greg's face lightened. "Really? I would appreciate that." Then, he paused, "Promise you'll talk to the sheriff first, though. I don't want you two getting hurt on my behalf."

Beth promised. She collected her books and headed toward the door. With her hand on the doorknob, she turned and said, "And you know what? Maybe we can throw a holiday party in here and try and raise some funds for the library, too."

Greg smiled and rose to his feet. "I would definitely be open to that," he said excitedly.

"Let me talk to Anna," Beth said. "I'll be back soon." She headed out the door and stepped out into the brisk cold air with only one thing on her mind. She couldn't wait to get home to talk to her sister.

It looked like they had another mystery to solve.

Ginger Carrot Cake Cinnamon Rolls with Cream Cheese Frosting

Dough:

1 package of dry yeast (¼ oz, not instant yeast)

½ cup warm water (as per yeast directions)

½ cup milk

¼ cup sugar

⅓ cup butter, melted

1 teaspoon salt

1 large egg

½ teaspoon cinnamon

¼ teaspoon ground nutmeg

1 ½ cups shredded carrot (approximately 3-4 carrots)

4 cups all-purpose flour

Filling:

4 tablespoons butter, melted

1 cup brown sugar

3 tablespoons cinnamon

1 teaspoon ground ginger

½ teaspoon ground nutmeg

⅛ teaspoon ground cloves

¾ cup walnuts, chopped (optional)

¼ cup candied ginger, chopped (optional)

Glaze:

3 tablespoons cream cheese

3 tablespoons milk

1 ½ cups powdered sugar

Candied ginger for decorating

Marzipan or candy carrots for decorating

In a small bowl, dissolve yeast in ½ cup warm water as per package directions.

In a large bowl, mix the milk, sugar, melted butter, salt, egg, ½ teaspoon cinnamon, and ¼ teaspoon nutmeg. Check temperature. Once temps are 110F or below, add yeast mixture and mix to combine.

Add in 2 cups of flour and shredded carrots. Mix until smooth. Add additional flour, ½ cup at a time until the dough is easy to handle.

Roll the dough out onto a floured surface and knead for 5-10 minutes.

Place the dough into a greased bowl, and cover with saran wrap topped with a kitchen towel. Let sit until dough has doubled in size, approximately 60-90 minutes.

When dough is doubled in size, punch it down. Then, roll dough into a rectangle approximately 9"x"15".

Spread the melted butter on top of the dough.

Mix the cinnamon, brown sugar, ground ginger, ground nutmeg, and ground cloves in a small bowl. Sprinkle the mixture over the butter. Sprinkle the candied ginger across the dough to your preference. Top with walnuts, if using.

From the long edge, tightly roll the dough all the way to the other long edge and pinch dough together to seal. Using a serrated knife, cut the log in half. Then cut each half into half again, creating a total of 4 pieces. Lining up two pieces at a time, cut each piece into 3. You should have a total of 12 pieces when finished cutting.

Coat the bottom of your 9"x13" baking pan with butter and sugar to coat. Place the cinnamon rolls in the place close together and let them rise until the dough has doubled again, approximately 45 minutes.

Preheat the oven to 350 degrees. Bake for about 30 minutes or until they are starting to brown.

While the rolls are baking, prepare the icing. Whisk the cream cheese in a stand mixer until creamy. Add the milk and whisk in until combined. Stir in the powdered sugar and whisk until smooth.

Pour the glaze over the rolls. Decorate with candied ginger or candy carrots, if desired. Serve warm.

This recipe was adapted from https://www.threeolivesbranch.com/.

Amish Pumpkin Pie Cake

129 ounce can of pumpkin puree (3 ½ cups)

¼ teaspoon salt

2 teaspoons cinnamon

½ teaspoon ground ginger

¼ teaspoon grated nutmeg

1 cup brown sugar

3 eggs

12 ounce can of evaporated milk

15 ounce box of yellow cake mix

½ cup butter, melted

1 cup chopped pecans

Preheat oven to 350 degrees. Grease a 9"x13" baking pan.

In a large bowl, whisk together pumpkin, salt, cinnamon, ginger, nutmeg, brown sugar, and eggs.

Add evaporated milk and blend. Pour mixture into pan.

Sift entire box of cake mix on top of pumpkin batter. Make sure the mix reaches to the edges of the pan. Pour melted butter on top.

Sprinkle chopped pecans over the top.

Bake for 50 minutes on center rack of oven. Cut into squares to serve.

Garnish with whipped cream if desired.

This recipe was adapted from https://12tomatoes.com/.

A Note from the Author

Thank you for reading *A Blessing in Disguise*. For some reason, this book took me much longer to write than I had planned. Maybe it was because it was met with holidays and family celebrations that were distracting, or maybe it was the actual story itself.

In the end, however, I found myself crying right along with Jessica, experiencing her fears as I typed.

I laughed at the innocent teasing that pops up off and on with Mark and the twins.

And I smiled throughout the entire last chapter, creating the Thanksgiving dinner scene.

Little Valley and all the characters in *The Amish Lantern Mystery Series* have become very real to me, and on one hand, it's hard to believe that this is only the fifth book in the series. On the other hand, it's so hard to believe that I have *already* written the fifth book in the series.

It's a strange and wonderful experience all at the same time, and I'm more than flattered that you choose to follow along with the stories that are born inside my mind.

Until next time... not unlike Anna and Beth, I sit with so much gratitude for you, for my family, for this wonderful adventure called life, and most of all, for imagination.

Warmest regards,
Mary B.

About Author

Mary B. Barbee is the author of the *Amish Lantern Mystery Series*. As an avid fan of all mystery and suspense in print, on television and in film, Mary B. believes the best mystery is one where the suspect changes throughout the story, keeping the audience guessing. She enjoys providing an exciting escape for a few hours with stories her readers can't put down - and always with a surprise ending.

When not writing, Mary B. is either playing a couple sets of tennis or a strategy board game with her two witty daughters and her kindly competitive mother. The four of them share a home in the Inland Northwest in the beautiful town of Spokane, Washington with their really cute - but sometimes naughty - chihuahua.

Mary loves to hear from her readers. Connect at:

marybbarbee@gmail.com

www.facebook.com/marybbarbee

Instagram @marybbarbee

www.marybbarbee.com

Made in the USA
Monee, IL
29 July 2022